Dear Reader,

During the eighteen years my husband and I and the kids lived in Austin, Texas, it snowed only twice—and melted the next day in both cases. So you can imagine our excitement our first winter in North Carolina, when we learned a major snowstorm was on the way. Unfortunately we couldn't have been less prepared. We had no rock salt or sand for the sidewalks, no shovel to clear them and perilously few supplies.

Gamely, we ran out to get milk, bread and a bag of rock salt. (We didn't get a shovel because we didn't really think we'd need one.) We put our eldest daughter on a plane back to college. And settled in for a few inches.

The "few inches" turned into the Blizzard of '96 delivered in three separate back-to-back storms that closed schools and businesses for a week. During that time, as my family and I struggled to dig our way out of the driveway with a garden shovel, a hoe, a rake and other assorted garden tools, I found myself doing plenty of daydreaming. What if a runaway bride, a schoolteacher on a fieldtrip and a young mother with her baby got stranded by the snowstorm, at the worst possible times, in the best possible places, with the men of their dreams? The result: Three new romantic comedies— SNOWBOUND BRIDE, HOT CHOCOLATE HONEYMOON and SNOW BABY.

I hope you enjoy reading all three books in my new trilogy, BRIDES, BABIES & BLIZZARDS, as much as I enjoyed writing them.

Best wishes, always,

Cathy Gillen Thacker

(who now has two shovels and a bag of rock salt, "just in case")

Cathy Gillen Thacker
HOT CHOCOLATE HONEYMOON

Harlequin Books

TORONTO • NEW YORK • LONDON
AMSTERDAM • PARIS • SYDNEY • HAMBURG
STOCKHOLM • ATHENS • TOKYO • MILAN
MADRID • WARSAW • BUDAPEST • AUCKLAND

ISBN 0-373-16717-2

HOT CHOCOLATE HONEYMOON

Chapter One

"I'm telling you I need a female agent sent down here to pose as my fiancée and I need one now!" Ryan McCoy groused over the secured telephone line.

"Why?" his boss, Juliet North, prodded. "What's going on?"

He kicked back in his chair, and propped his boot-clad feet on the corner of his desk. "Let's just say that since Christmas came and went with no sign of the future Mrs. Ryan McCoy I've had more offers to cook a meal and darn my socks than I can handle."

"Hmm." Juliet—who was very happily married herself—paused. She continued with mock seriousness, "Did you try singing them one of your love songs?"

"Very funny," Ryan said dryly. "And for your information, yes, I have, to no avail. The local women couldn't care less about my pronounced inability to write an intelligible lyric or carry a tune." Portable phone in hand, Ryan stood and stalked restlessly across the secret cave in the side of the mountain. Scowling, he glanced through the high-powered telescope in front of him. He noted the wind picking up and the snow coming down in ever-increasing intensity to the point where he couldn't even see the area targeted for surveillance.

Juliet chuckled on the other end of the line, while Ryan checked the visual on the local weather radar on his computer screen. Just as he had feared, the storm, now being dubbed The Snowstorm of the Century— predicted to rival the Blizzard of '96—was heading relentlessly up the East Coast and into Virginia, where it was expected to dump a record snowfall. It had only been snowing an hour or so, but they already had several inches on the ground, with two dozen more or so predicted to come in the next twenty-four hours. He could only guess how that was going to hamper his ongoing investigation.

"What *do* the local women care about, then?" Juliet asked.

Ryan sighed as he thanked heaven for underground utilities and poured himself another cup of Swiss almond coffee. "My future romantic happiness. And, for the record, just about everyone in these parts is beginning to question my fidelity to a beautiful fiancée no one's ever seen. Of course, if I could pinpoint an *exact time* when the future Mrs. Ryan McCoy might show up, it might help take some of the pressure off."

"I'd love to send you someone to kiss and cuddle. But you know how few female agents we have available to be reassigned right now."

"Meaning no go?" Ryan guessed dejectedly as he raked a hand through his rumpled hair.

"Not for the next month, anyway," Juliet confirmed.

Ryan swore heatedly as he lifted his coffee cup to his lips. "You know how many women I'm going to have to fend off in the meantime, don't you?"

"I have no control over that. It's your fault for being so darned handsome!"

"Hey," Ryan said defensively. He was a little embarrassed at all the unsolicited female attention he'd been receiving. "I've done my best to appear lazy, deluded and unsuccessful."

"Or in other words," Juliet paraphrased dryly, "a poor catch."

"A very poor catch," Ryan confirmed, then sighed as he sifted through a stack of the last surveillance photos taken and developed via machine. "It's not my fault this particular area of Virginia has a dearth of eligible men and a wealth of attractive, highly eligible women."

"Well, stay goofily ineligible a little while longer, will you?" Juliet prodded. "We need to get this assignment wrapped up."

Ryan caught the new edge in Juliet's voice and knew something vital was up. "Something happen?"

Juliet paused. "Our intelligence in Rivertown has picked up a possible shipment."

Ryan's broad shoulders tensed beneath his navy blue thermal underwear and thick flannel shirt. "When?"

"Probably by the end of the week, even with the weather."

Ryan looked at the surveillance monitor again and scowled at the dense gray-white clouds on the horizon. More activity on the Hindale farm was the last thing they needed during a winter storm that was quickly paralyzing the whole Eastern Seaboard. "How soon after that do you expect them to act?" Ryan demanded impatiently.

"A matter of days. Maybe even hours." Juliet paused. "Naturally we hope to avoid any type of armed confrontation with their group. It's all going to depend on what kind of visuals you can get us to take forward."

Ryan's blood pumped as he anticipated the challenge to come. There was no one he wanted to put out of business more than this group, whom he considered to be as dangerous as they came, but to do that he needed the kind of proof that would stand up in court. "I'll get it," he promised grimly, checking to make sure his high-powered cameras were loaded with both film and videotape. Satisfied all was in order, he continued, "But in return, you owe me a favor."

Juliet chuckled, not the least surprised to be put on notice by him. "Which is..."

"As soon as I'm finished, I want out of here, that second," Ryan demanded as he looked out the telescope and turned his attention to the road. To his amazement he saw a dark blue Suburban four-by-four pulled to one side of the precariously curving, two-lane mountain road leading to his farmhouse. Judging by the rather odd way it was listing to one side, the vehicle looked disabled. Even more incredible, a trim young blonde, clad in a city skirt and blazer, was climbing down out of the driver's seat, into the snow.

"You're not going to believe this," Ryan murmured appreciatively, his glance running over her slender form, and zeroing in on the thick, dark tights that encompassed a truly sensational pair of legs. "But I may soon have company."

"From across the valley?"

"No," Ryan said, as his heartbeat picked up and his mouth went dry, "the road. A stranded motorist."

"Well, get rid of him," Juliet advised, sounding just as irritated as Ryan should've felt. "Pronto, before you're stuck with an uninvited guest for the duration of the blizzard."

"He's a she," Ryan said, zooming in as close as possible and watching as the sumptuous-looking blonde—who still hadn't bothered to pull on a coat—tromped around the front of her truck. Her snowy white blouse was buttoned up as far as it would go, with some sort of glinting gold brooch pinned at the throat. Wispy bangs grazed her forehead, and she had her golden-blond hair pinned up in some sort of old-fashioned topknot that seemed to be losing strands to the blowing wind even as he spoke. Her cheeks were high, classically sculpted and pink, her lips bow-shaped, delicate and full.

"I'll do my best," Ryan promised, wondering why he didn't have a woman this attractive chasing him. "But it may not be possible in this weather," he finished honestly.

"Listen to me," Juliet fumed on the other end, "I

don't care if you *have* been without a woman damn near on a year, the last thing you need on the premises at this point is a damsel in distress.''

Not to mention a pretty, delicate-looking blonde who made his blood race just looking at her. Ryan swore, knowing the last thing he wanted to do was put some unsuspecting citizen in danger. "Like I don't know that?'' Ryan grumbled, realizing Juliet was right, the last thing he needed was to be distracted.

But damned if she wasn't the prettiest thing he'd seen in a heck of a long time, he thought as he watched the stranded woman hunker down beside the right-front tire.

"I KNEW IT! We're not only so lost we'll never find our way back, we're all going to die!'' ten-year-old Greta wailed as Grace Tennessen opened the door to the Suburban truck and climbed behind the steering wheel.

"No, we're not, silly,'' Hannah, the fourteen-year-old, replied as Grace swiveled around to face them.

"Listen up, girls,'' she announced to the group of seven Peach Blossom Academy students, aged six to fourteen, in her care. "Everyone grab their coats, hats and mittens, and make sure you have your snow boots on because we're all going to take a hike.''

"In this snow?'' seven-year-old Brianna whimpered fearfully, sticking her thumb in her mouth and sucking furiously.

Grace gave the most fearful of her charges a little hug. "We have no choice, honey,'' she said. "The truck has a flat tire, and we're going to have to find someone to help us get it fixed." *Before the snow gets any worse, and we find ourselves in real danger,* Grace amended silently to herself. Determined, however, to present only a serenely confident attitude to the seven students she was shepherding, she shrugged her own coat on, tugged on her insulated leather driving gloves, climbed back out of the truck, and helped all the girls down, one by one.

"Where are we going?" twelve-year-old Darlene asked seriously.

The only place they could go, Grace thought. She pointed behind them, to the top of the snow-covered rise they'd passed a quarter mile down the winding mountain road. "You see that big farmhouse up on the hill back there?"

"That's not a h-h-hill, Ms. Tennessen," six-year-old Letticia stuttered, "That's a m-m-mountain!"

"Well, whatever it is, we're going to walk up there and telephone for help," Grace continued, already taking the lead.

"How long do you think it will take to get a tow truck in this weather, Miss Tennessen?" Clara, who was eight, asked.

Grace hadn't a clue, but she kept a cheerful outlook for the sake of the girls. "Not long. Now everyone hold hands and stay together. That's it." She smiled bravely. "We'll be there in no time, you'll see."

GRACE STOOD FACING the two-story farmhouse with the half new, half old pale yellow paint and pine green shutters. No one had answered her knock, and she was doing her best not to express her concern to the children.

"Hey, look. There's smoke coming from the chimney," Polly, nine, said as she nervously tugged on her pigtails and regarded the half-repainted home.

"Then how come they aren't answering the door?" Greta demanded grumpily, pushing her snow-dusted glasses up on the bridge of her nose.

"I dunno." Clara shrugged as they all gathered around on the covered front porch.

"Perhaps they're somewhere else, and stuck in the snow, too," Hannah, the oldest, suggested, as she leaned against the railing, shivering in the blowing snow and biting cold.

Her breath making frosty circles in the air, Darlene demanded, "What do you think, Ms. Tennessen?"

That we are in a heap of trouble, Grace thought as she put on her most confident expression. "Perhaps they didn't hear us. We'll knock a little louder." She rapped loudly and distinctly five times, and heard nothing but the wind howling through the pines in response. The opaque white curtains blocking the view of the interior did not shift in the slightest. And then the girls all spoke at once.

"I'm cold."

"I'm freezing, too."

"Are we going to have to walk all the way back to the truck?"

"I don't think I can make it, if that's the case."

"I'm really, r-r-really c-c-cold, Ms. Tennessen."

Desperate times called for desperate measures. Grace drew a bolstering breath and went ahead and tried the door. Damn, it was locked. Maybe a window—somewhere—had been left unlocked. Surely the owners wouldn't mind if they took shelter, under the circumstances. "Stay right here, girls. Out of the wind. Yes, that's it. I'm going to go around to the back and see if there's another door there."

Brianna took her thumb out of her mouth long enough to ask. "You won't leave and forget us?"

"Of course not." Grace gave her a reassuring hug. "I'm going to do my best to get us warm as soon as possible. All right?"

Brianna and the rest of the girls nodded.

Grace tromped down the porch steps and around to the back door. She rapped again, very loudly and received no reply. "Hello?" she called cheerily, peering through the glass. She could see a kitchen, but no signs of life. "Anybody in there? Anyone at all?" Hearing no response, she tried the door. It, too, was locked. Praying she wouldn't be mistaken for a burglar, she tried the window. It was locked, and so was every other window.

By the time she circled the rambling farmhouse and reached the girls again, she knew what she had to do. "I'm going to have to try and jimmy the lock," she told them as she removed her American Express gold card from her purse.

"Really?"

"Cool!"

Grace doubted the headmistress at The Peach Blossom Academy for Young Women would see it that way. "Now, it goes without saying you are all never to try this yourselves. Understood?" Grace said sternly.

"Yes, Ms. Tennessen," the group replied dutifully in unison. But their expressions were excited nevertheless as she carefully fitted her credit card in the slot of the door and used it to lift the lock ever so slightly, hearing a very tiny, very satisfying *click* as it slid back into its housing.

Grace turned the knob, the door swung open, and she led the girls in.

"AND I THOUGHT our dormitory rooms were a mess!" Darlene exclaimed in awe as the group surveyed the large front room, complete with untidy heaps of dust-covered books, clothing, sports equipment. A huge state-of-the-art stereo system, big-screen TV, and a single well-worn lounge chair were surrounded by sliding stacks of compact discs and videotapes.

"Who lives here, anyway?" Clara asked.

Greta looked around the room in awe. "I've never seen so many posters of country-and-western singers in one place!"

"Is that s-s-supposed to be Elvis?" Letticia asked with a perplexed frown.

"What's 'Hee Haw'?" Hannah asked, pointing to a framed picture of a lady with a price tag hanging off her hat. "'Cause there's a poster of that, too."

"I never heard of anyone having a ceramic statue

of a sleeping dog next to their fireplace,'' Darlene observed.

Polly stifled a sneeze as she pointed to the statue, too. "Do you think whoever lives here made that himself?"

"No," Grace murmured, momentarily as awestruck as the girls as—without touching anything—she looked high and low for a telephone she might borrow. "They sell them at the stores in the malls. I've seen them."

"He must like watching sports on TV, too." Brianna pointed to the television guide to the satellite sports channels.

"He's even got a basketball hoop on the wall over there," Greta announced, impressed. "From the marks on the wall around it, it looks like he's been shooting a real basketball inside the house!"

Grace looked up and with chagrin admitted to herself that was true.

Clara frowned, perplexed. "How do you know it's a guy who lives here?" she asked.

Hannah rolled her eyes. "Look at the size of that shirt and those boots. Those are men's clothes. Besides, I don't see any girly things around here, do you?"

Grace's heart pounded. The girls were right. Those clothes that were heaped all over the place were made for a very tall, muscular man. Furthermore, there were no possessions that indicated either a woman or youngsters of any kind lived here. What exactly had she stumbled into? And what would the man who owned this farmhouse think when he returned to find his turf had been invaded by a schoolteacher and seven little girls on a field trip? She could not imagine he would be too pleased. And with good reason.

Grace regarded her charges sternly. "Girls, we mustn't snoop. It's bad enough we had to jimmy the door and come in here uninvited. Now, everyone come over here and sit by the fire. That's it, form a semi-circle. I want you all to stay warm while I see—" she turned toward the highly disorganized stacks of his belongings and began lifting them gingerly as she continued "—about finding a phone to call for help."

"Well now, isn't this interesting," a deep male voice rumbled in a honeyed Southern drawl as a shadow fell over Grace and the girls. Her stomach plummeting at the sound of that smooth, sexy voice, Grace looked up. And saw one of the most ruggedly handsome, powerfully built men she'd ever encountered in her life. He was tall, at least six feet five inches, with broad, imposing shoulders and long, lean legs. Beneath the soft worn jeans and flannel shirt, he was solidly muscled from head to toe. Rumpled golden-brown hair—windswept and dotted with snowflakes—fell rakishly across his brow, the tops of his ears and the back of his neck. But, to her immense relief, instead of being ticked off to find her and the girls in his home uninvited, his golden-brown eyes were alight with mischief and a distinctly sexual, distinctly masculine appreciation of her.

Shivers that had absolutely nothing to do with the cold raced up and down Grace's spine. "Um—I can explain," Grace murmured as his sensually chiseled lips turned up in a faintly knowing, faintly challenging smile. "I'm Grace Tennessen, a history instructor at The Peach Blossom Academy for Young Women in Arlington, Virginia."

He looked her up and down as the corners of his mouth curled up. "You're quite a ways from there," he noted, folding his arms in front of him.

Clear across the state, as a matter of fact, Grace thought.

"We got lost," Hannah piped up helpfully.

"Yeah," Darlene added, for a moment putting the calculator she liked to carry with her aside. "The detour signs said this was the way to I-81, but it's not."

He looked sympathetic, but not surprised as his eyes drifted over Grace again, lingering on her face and hair. "The teenagers in the area have been turning around road signs to throw off unsuspecting motorists."

"Well, it worked." Grace sighed unhappily as his glance drifted lower still. "Because we sure headed off on the wrong road in the wrong direction."

"And then it started snowing," Greta said.

"And we g-g-got a flat tire—" Letticia added.

"And here we are," Clara piped up.

Grace reddened again, and with one hand, self-consciously tried to restore order to her hair. "Again, I apologize for bursting in on you like this—"

"How *did* you get in, by the way?" he asked pleasantly.

"American Express." Grace slipped the gold card

out of her pocket and held it up for him to see as she quipped, "I never leave home without it."

To her relief he looked amused, rather than angry. "I can see where it came in real handy."

"Yes, well, I wouldn't have barged in if I hadn't been desperate to use the phone to call the auto club. So if you don't mind—"

Nodding his agreement, he looked around and finally tugged a combination phone and answering machine out from beneath a pile of newspapers. "Be my guest," he said, unraveling the cord and handing the entire unit over.

"Thank you," Grace said.

The base of the phone in one hand, the receiver in the other, Grace dialed the 800 number of the auto club. She explained her problem, then frowned at the answer. "Well?" the handsome stranger prodded when she had ended the call with a push of the button.

Grace sighed her disappointment and relayed what she'd been told. "They're swamped. Every tow truck available is already out on calls, and they have a waiting list over four hours long as it stands. Considering the way it's snowing in most parts of the state, they can't guarantee me help until much later tonight—if then, depending on the state of the roads." Which meant she had to get herself and the girls out of here, fast, before they really did get stuck here.

"So what next?" he asked, beginning to look a little worried, too.

There were a lot of people counting on her. Grace wasn't about to let them down. Grace squared her shoulders determinedly. "Just what you'd think. I take care of this problem the old-fashioned way and change the tire without the auto club's help." She turned her attention back to the phone in her hand. "First, however, I'd better call the school and let them know we're all right. I was supposed to call hours ago to let them know we'd arrived at our destination, and given the weather, they're probably worried sick."

While he picked up an acoustic guitar that had been polished to a golden sheen, propped it gently in his arms and settled it on the edge of a nearby desk, Grace placed a collect call. She got hold of the headmistress and swiftly explained the problem, only to be promptly—and infuriatingly—told it might be best to just stay put. "We can't do that," Grace said firmly, aware the handsome stranger whose house she had just broken into was covertly listening to her every word.

"Why not?" the headmistress demanded in her usual exacting tone.

Grace turned her glance away from the stranger and studied the snow coming down outside. Thank heaven he regarded them as a pleasant diversion and not an infuriating nuisance. "This is a private residence, not a hotel." *And he's too damned attractive.* "I'm sure we can make it to a hotel before the roads become impassable. In the meantime, just so the school knows, where exactly are we, Mr.—"

"McCoy. Ryan McCoy. And you're at 100 High Mountain Road in Blue Mountain Gap, Virginia." He relayed the phone number.

Grace repeated the information for the headmistress.

"Tell your boss not to worry," Ryan offered as he idly strummed a few chords. "I'll make sure you all get where you need to go."

"Thank you," Grace murmured, beginning to relax just a tad as she conveyed his promise to the school. She glanced at her watch, aware valuable time was passing. She needed to get a move on if she was going to make good on her promise. "Yes, I'll call as soon as we get settled somewhere for the night. All right. Goodbye." She hung up the phone, then paused as she looked down. "Your message light is blinking."

He nodded, unconcerned, as his eyes drifted over her in a way that warmed her frozen body from head to toe. "So it is."

Grace flushed with awareness despite herself. "Aren't you going to check and see what it is?"

He regarded her with guileless eyes and a deceptively innocent smile as he lazily waved off her suggestion. "Nah, I don't usually listen to my messages."

Grace narrowed her eyes at him. She suspected he was a lot more ambitious than he was pretending to be. And that this good-old-boy charm of his was a device he used to keep people at arm's length, without going so far as to be rude or unsociable. "Then why do you have an answering machine?" she asked calmly.

He flashed her a smile that upped her pulse another notch and sent her stomach plummeting. He set his guitar aside and said, "So phone calls won't interrupt me."

"Let me get this straight," Grace said finally, in a

low, stymied voice, while Ryan noted that she was even lovelier up close than she had been through the lens of his telescope.

"You have a phone you'd just as soon not answer, and an answering machine that takes messages you never check."

"That about sums it up," Ryan drawled, resisting the urge to touch her silky blond hair and soft, fair skin or drown in the depths of her jade green eyes. His boss had been right; this woman was a distraction he didn't need, he thought as the seven lively looking little girls in private school uniforms of tartan plaid skirts, navy blazers and berets and matching dress-length wool coats continued to regard him with the same wide-eyed bemusement as their teacher.

"Then why do you even have a phone?" she persisted primly.

Ryan gave a hapless shrug and stuck his fingers in the front pockets of his jeans. He didn't know what it was about this pretty twenty-something schoolteacher, but he found himself wanting to get under her skin in the worst way. "For emergencies, like now. 'Course, if my luck changes and I actually get a song or two published," he drawled with an ingratiating wink, "I may need to start answering my phone."

"You write songs?" one of the girls interjected with a breathless excitement apparently not shared by her teacher.

Ryan smiled down at the little girl kindly, aware how much he had missed being around his own nieces and nephews the past year. One of the first things he was going to do when he finished his undercover assignment was go and see them. "Yep, and as a matter of fact, I got a number of songs I'm working on right now."

But unlike the other females in the area, their teacher did not want to hear about his songwriting talent, or, more accurately, Ryan thought, lack thereof. "Look, I hate to ask," she said, capturing his attention once again, "but if we're to get out of here swiftly, I'm going to need your help changing the tire on my truck."

Ryan folded his arms in front of him and regarded her drolly. As their eyes locked, he could almost feel the shields go up around her. Shields he was determined to tear down. "Let me get this straight," he said, mocking her earlier words. "You expect me to hike all the way down to the road and help you do that in this snowstorm?"

"It's not snowing that badly yet," she replied coolly, with the pleasant schoolteacher demeanor of someone used to having her every wish carried out without question. "And yes, I do."

"Uh-huh." He folded his arms in front of him and looked her up and down, wondering when the last time was she'd heard a no, wondering just what it was about her that piqued his interest so much. Wondering what it would take to get her to feel the same. "And what are you going to do for me in return?"

Chapter Two

Knowing it was imperative she get the upper hand—now—before their repartee got any more out of hand, Grace pretended not to understand what this hot-blooded country Romeo was hinting at.

Smiling up at him sweetly, she pledged in her most-pleasant tone, "If you like, after you assist me, I'll pay you for your time and trouble."

Laugh lines crinkled at the corners of his golden-brown eyes as his glance leisurely roved her lips. Grace knew right then and there that Ryan McCoy was everything her mother had warned her about—and more.

His glance still focused on her thoughtfully, he leaned toward her and whispered in a lascivious tone just loud enough for her to hear. "I appreciate your wanting to compensate me, but just so you and I are on the same page—that is most definitely not the kind of thank-you I had in mind."

Grace flushed. He wasn't being as cooperative as she had hoped, but she had enough experience dealing with difficult parents and administrators to think that, given a little time and opportunity, she could handle him, anyway.

Wary of her students overhearing anything they shouldn't, Grace pointed toward the front door and spoke in her coolest, most-authoritative voice. "Let's you and I take this outside, shall we?"

Ryan sighed loudly. "Well, girls," he drawled with a rueful shake of his head. He slapped his hands on his hips. "Looks like I've been sent to the principal's office again."

The girls giggled in chorus, anxious to see what the handsome bounder was going to do next.

"Now, Mr. McCoy!" Grace stressed with a decided lack of patience as she pointed the way. She knew they were providing the girls with much more entertainment than warranted. And worse, that Ryan McCoy was the kind of good old boy not above saying just about anything to wring a laugh from those around him.

Ryan winked at his young audience before sauntering in the direction Grace pointed. "You know," he said, grabbing the snow-flecked down jacket he'd tossed aside as he'd come in and shrugging it over his broad shoulders in one smooth motion. "You have a surprisingly commanding voice for such a dainty little woman."

Stunned at how quickly he'd made her feel way out of her league, Grace drew a bolstering breath and stiffened her spine. "I advise you not to underestimate me, Mr. McCoy, because I am not dainty and I am not little," Grace replied, irritated. She stood five foot seven in her bare feet and weighed exactly what she should for her height and age. It was just he was so darn tall and muscular that next to him she seemed little.

"Feminine then," he amended, as their eyes clashed and held. A heat wave, completely at odds with the frigid temperatures outside, swept through her.

"I think he's trying to pay you a compliment, Ms. Tennessen," Hannah said helpfully.

Grace sent an officious smile toward her charges as Ryan reached past her to get the door. "I know what he's trying to do, girls," she told them, as she inhaled the wintry scent of his cologne. *He's trying to get under my skin. Unfortunately, it was working, because her heart had never thudded so hard or so fast, just being near someone.* Aware she felt inexplicably giddy and unaccountably nervous, she said, "While I take care of the tire, I want you girls to stay here where it's warm. Hannah and Darlene, you two are the oldest, so you're in charge."

Reassured her students were going to be fine in her absence, Grace followed Ryan outside and shut the door behind him. They moved down to the far end of the front porch, as far out of earshot as possible. "I cannot believe you said what you did in there."

He grinned, delighted, and continued to regard her like a puppy dog happily anticipating his next meal. "Oh, lighten up. It wasn't all that bad."

Says who, Grace wondered, aware she had a reputation to maintain. "The way you looked at me just then—"

"Yes?" he said, baiting her.

She knew she had to say it if she wanted to avoid further embarrassment or entanglement. "It was suggestive."

He pressed his hands to his chest in an affronted gesture and was suddenly all youthful innocence. "Hey, you don't know what I had in mind in exchange for helping you with your tire."

Grace gave him a deadpan glance. Maybe not, but her lips were still tingling from the heat of his look, her pulse still racing from the unfathomable quality in his golden-brown eyes. "Then suppose you enlighten me," she prodded dryly.

"Good idea." He flashed a lady-killer grin, took her elbow gallantly in hand and led her gently off the porch. "But while we're talking, we'd better head on down and get that tire changed before this snowstorm gets any worse."

Watching the huge white flakes swirl around them, Grace couldn't argue with that. She had the feeling this man was dangerous to her heart, and the husky undertone of sexual innuendo in his voice was just the beginning. She fixed a bright smile on her face. "Fine, but I'm not letting you off the hook for what you said. The girls' parents would be horrified if they'd overheard any of that!"

"And don't forget," he said, an expression of amusement flickering across his face, "you are, too."

"With good reason," Grace replied, hating the fact he made her feel every inch the ice princess she had long been reputed to be.

"Just out of curiosity," he asked, as they set off down the long narrow drive edged with stands of pine. "You always been this prissy, or just since becoming a schoolteacher?"

Grace knew exactly what had frozen her blood, where men were concerned, but she was not about to discuss that chain of events with him. She shoved her gloved hands in the pockets of her coat and set her chin. "Let's just keep our mind on the task, shall we?"

The corners of his mouth curled up. "I annoy you, don't I?"

Let me count the ways. "I admit I was hoping to find a gentleman and a phone at your farmhouse."

"And instead you found only half of what you wanted."

Grace shrugged as if unconcerned. "That seems to be the way my luck is running today. And while we are on the subject of your behavior, Mr. McCoy—"

"Were we?"

"I will not have the girls subjected to reckless behavior they might be tempted to emulate."

His eyes pierced straight through her. "Don't you mean suggestive?"

"That, Mr. McCoy, is exactly the kind of unwarranted remark I am talking about, and I will not tolerate it!"

"May I remind you that this is my property you're on, and my rules, and I did not ask for your company! Furthermore, as I indicated to you back up at the house, I'm not in the habit of doing something for nothing.''

Grace's heart stalled in her chest. Suddenly she had a tiger by the tail. ''What are you suggesting?''

''Don't go getting your knickers in a knot. It's nothing that bad. Just a favor for a favor.''

''What kind of favor?'' Grace stopped walking and regarded him suspiciously.

He took her arm and propelled her forward again. ''I just want you to hug me and make a big show of saying goodbye to me before you and the girls take off for parts unknown.''

Grace whirled toward him, stunned. ''Why would I want to do that?''

He shrugged offhandedly and flashed another lady-killer grin. ''Because you're grateful for my assistance and one good turn deserves another?''

Grace was no fool; she knew it was more than that. They reached the road and turned in the direction of her truck. Their boots made soft, crunching noises on the snow-covered road. ''What are you really trying to pull here?'' she demanded.

''A fast one, obviously.''

''Why?'' Grace protested. And why tell her that?

Ryan grimaced. ''Because I need a little peace and quiet.''

Grace blinked as they reached her truck and circled around the front. ''And a hug from me—in public—will give you that?'' she demanded, leaning against the bumper.

He leaned against the bumper, too. ''Maybe.''

Grace's jaw set. As far as she was concerned, there was nothing to think about. "No. I'm not going to be party to any sort of ruse."

He regarded her with exasperation as snow continued to dust his broad shoulders. "Look, I don't like this any more than you do."

"Then why are you asking me to do it?" Grace demanded.

Amazingly calm and laid-back under the circumstances, he knelt to examine her flat tire. "Because I don't have any choice," he said, as if what he was asking were no big deal.

"That may be true," Grace countered, upset, "but I do have a choice, Mr. McCoy."

"Ryan."

"And I choose not to get involved in any sort of con—"

He straightened abruptly. "Even if you owe me big-time for helping you out, and you'd be doing me a huge favor?"

Grace studied him. As much as she was loath to admit it, there was something earnest and worthwhile in his face. "Maybe you should just start from the beginning," she urged, hoping there was a very good reason behind his request.

Ryan walked to the back of her truck. "I came up here to get some peace and quiet."

"Which you seem to have in abundance," Grace commented as she unlocked the back and opened the cargo doors.

Ryan opened the tire well and pulled out the spare,

jack and lug wrench. "To keep the women away, I invented a future Mrs. Ryan McCoy."

"Only there is no future Mrs. Ryan McCoy," Grace guessed.

"Right." Ryan carried all three items to the front of the truck and set them down in the snow. "And now people are beginning to get suspicious."

A pulse beat of silence stretched between them. Grace paced back and forth as Ryan swiftly jacked up her vehicle. "Why not tell them the truth?"

Ryan fit the wrench around the first lug nut. "And have the locals trying to get me married off right and left to one of the kazillion single women in the area? No way. I don't need that kind of aggravation in my life right now."

"Not the marrying kind?" Grace prodded, not sure why that knowledge should irritate her, yet knowing it did.

"You wanted the truth," he said flatly as he deposited the lug nut on top of her truck. "I'm giving it." He paused again and regarded her quietly. "If I didn't need your help as desperately as you need mine, I wouldn't ask."

"So, in other words, you want me to pretend I'm your fiancée."

"It'd help me out a lot if you'd leave people with that impression."

"I told you before—I do not want to be party to any sort of con game."

"I'm not asking you to," he continued sternly. "I just want you to give me a hug or two in public, and then people can jump to whatever assumptions they choose to jump to on their own. If any fibbing is required, and for the record I sincerely hope to heaven none is, I'll do it.''

He made it all sound so easy, but Grace had learned the hard way that even the best-laid plans had a habit of going awry. Plus, she was a teacher on a field trip, and she had an example to set for her students. ''Forget it.''

''That decision cuts both ways, lady.'' He opened her hand and folded the lug wrench into it.

Grace tried not to think how firm and strong his touch was, as she stared at him, aghast. ''What are you doing?'' she asked hoarsely.

He shrugged. ''Easy. If you're not going to help me, I won't help you.''

''Fine.'' Grace scowled, hunkered down beside the tire, and fit the tool over the lug nut. She put as much pressure on the wrench as she could—to no avail. The lug nut didn't budge. Not about to give up, she tried another lug nut. To her frustration, it was just as immovable. ''Whoever put these on here tightened them way too much,'' Grace muttered in aggravation. *Although,* a tiny voice inside her said, *he'd had no problem loosening and removing one.*

Ryan squatted beside her, his gloved hands resting lightly against the insides of his muscular, denim-clad thighs. ''Ready to cry uncle yet?''

Her pride said no. Her practical side said maybe she had better think about this again.

Like it or not, when it came to changing tires, Grace

knew she was no pro under the best of circumstances. In the time it had taken for her to get his help, another inch of snow had fallen on the ground. Given the fact she was an experienced driver in all kinds of weather and had four-wheel-drive on her truck, she could still make it down the mountain and into town, but only if she got started again before the road became impassable.

Of course, she could wait for another driver to render aid. But that wasn't very likely, as she had yet to see another vehicle on this deserted mountain road.

She shivered in the blowing wind. It was killing her to have to give in. But what choice did she have? She tipped her face up to his. "You swear to me my students won't hear a word about our bargain?"

"Cross my heart."

With a groan of resignation, she handed the lug wrench to him. "Fine. I'll do what you want. You win."

"Great." His expression one of supreme satisfaction, Ryan swiftly went to work. In two minutes he had the rest of the lug nuts and the damaged tire off. He paused to examine it and was quickly able to point out the problem. "You've got a nail in it."

So Grace saw. "Is there anyplace close by I could get the tire patched?" she asked. She could drive on her spare, but it was smaller than the other tires, and made for a rough, slow ride.

"Actually, I could do it. I've got a kit up in the barn," Ryan said as the slow, rumbling sound of a truck motor had them both turning. As he noted the vintage pickup truck on jacked-up wheels, the muscles in Ryan's jaw turned rigid and he swore beneath his breath.

"Someone you know?" Grace asked grimly.

"Fred Hindale," Ryan replied tersely. "He owns a farm across the valley."

"So?" Grace whispered as the noisy truck came closer.

"I don't have time to explain," Ryan said urgently as they both got to their feet. "Just follow my lead and let me do the talking," he warned grimly.

As the pickup came even with them, Ryan draped a possessive arm about Grace's shoulders. Fred Hindale stuck his head out the pickup window and looked Grace up and down. "Well, now," he drawled in a cruelly insinuating tone as he flashed a leering grin at Grace and stroked his whisker-stubbled chin. Hindale turned his glance back to Ryan. "Don't tell me your woman finally showed up to pay you a visit. And all these weeks after Christmas, too."

The way Hindale was looking at them both made the hair on the back of Grace's neck stand on end. Ryan flashed an easy grin that belied none of the anxiety Grace was feeling. "And here we were hoping to keep it a secret," Ryan joked.

Hindale inclined his head toward the back of his truck. A net was strung across the bed of the pickup. Beneath it were a dozen or more sacks of groceries, several cases of beer, two bags of rock salt and half a dozen plain brown jugs that might have held anything from homemade cider to whiskey. "I just came from town. They were in the process of closing the bridges between here and there—they're already icing up. So I hope you've laid your supplies in, 'cause it looks like none of us will be getting off this mountain until the storm passes.''

Panic welled inside Grace. This was exactly what she did not need to happen. But it appeared the situation was already out of her hands.

''Hear that darlin'?'' Ryan said before she could comment, his grip on her shoulders tightening with a warm male possessiveness that both thrilled and stunned her. ''We're gonna be snowed in.'' One hand slipping behind her neck, he tugged her nearer, bent his head and touched his lips to hers. She uttered a soft oh of surprise that was promptly swallowed by the pressure of his mouth on hers, and then he gave her a slow, sensual kiss that stamped her as his and promised soul-shattering excitement in a way no words ever could have. Grace sagged against him, feeling stunned, thrilled and incredibly aroused. When he finally lifted his head from hers, she was breathing erratically and trembling from head to toe.

Hindale continued to regard them with more than the usual amount of curiosity. ''Seems like you two have missed each other,'' he said finally.

''More than we could ever put into words,'' Ryan murmured, running his hand down her cheek and looking at Grace as though the kiss had been every bit as glorious for him as it had been for her.

Hindale chuckled. ''Maybe you could write a song about it,'' he said contemptuously. He lifted his hand

and shifted back into gear. The jacked-up pickup rumbled away in a dark cloud of exhaust.

Grace waited until the truck had rounded the curve and disappeared from view before she swung back to Ryan. "Listen, country boy, I consented to a public hug in town. I did not say you could kiss me here in the middle of the road."

Ryan shrugged, looking like he half expected to be slugged. "I stand corrected."

But Grace had the feeling he wasn't sorry at all that he'd kissed her. Aware her pulse was still racing madly, and that there was a heck of a lot more going on here than Ryan McCoy had disclosed, she continued to study him. Was it her imagination, or had he thought the two of them were in some sort of danger just now? "You don't like that guy, do you?" she said, as prickles of unease danced along her skin.

Ryan shrugged and didn't answer. "Do you?"

The truth? The way Hindale had leered at her had given her the creeps.

"But enough about Hindale," Ryan continued firmly, determined to change the subject as he got back to the business at hand. "You and I have more serious things to discuss."

Grace jerked in a breath, wondering what the country Romeo was going to suggest now. "Such as?"

"With the bridges iced over, there's no way you and your students can get to town. And there are only two places to stay on this mountain."

"Don't tell me," Grace interjected, already finding it difficult to catch her breath. "Your place—"

"And the Hindale farm." Ryan sighed, looking as loath to face the music as she was. He shoved a hand through his hair, scattering snowflakes every which way, and continued curtly, "Whether either of us like it or not, you and the girls are going to have to stay with me until the blizzard lets up."

Chapter Three

"You're aggravated with me," Grace said several minutes later, as Ryan finished changing the tire and lowered the truck to the ground.

Actually, Ryan thought, as he shoved the jack, the lug wrench and the ruined tire back in the trunk, it was himself he was ticked off at. Because, more than anyone's, it was his fault she was going to be stuck here with him for the duration of the blizzard. He should've hurried her along, changed her tire quickly himself and led her and her charges down off the mountain without taking time to chat or make any deals. But he hadn't. Why? Because he was incredibly attracted to her. And that attraction had led to a kiss that damn well could and should have been avoided.

Since it hadn't been, he was going to have to do anything and everything he could to keep her at arm's length for the next few days.

Ryan shrugged as he strode around to the driver's side of the four-by-four and hopped in, leaving her to climb unassisted into the passenger side of her own vehicle. "I guess I'd just like to know what kind of teacher takes a bunch of innocent kids out in weather like this.'' He shot her an accusatory glance.

Taken aback by his criticism, Grace flushed. ''For your information I did not know it was supposed to snow this afternoon!''

Ryan turned on the front and rear windshield wipers and thrust the gear shift into reverse. ''And how the heck is that possible?'' he accused as he maneuvered the truck onto the road and backed up until he was in a position to turn into his own driveway.

''I listened to the weather report last night before I went to bed and again this morning before we left the inn where we stayed the night. They said the severe weather would not hit Virginia until Monday evening at the earliest. That gave me all day to get back on the interstate and get to our next stop in our tour of historic Virginia.''

Ryan was amused to realize she was as testy as he was at the thought that they were going to be snowed in together. ''You were listening to the radio, I take it?'' he questioned as he drove aggressively up the steep driveway.

Grace gripped the armrest and door handle tightly as she sent him a seething glance. ''Yes. A little transistor. The bed and breakfast inn did not have televisions. That was one of the things I liked about it.''

Ryan scowled as he drove up to the barn, where his own disreputable two-passenger Jeep was parked. He stopped in front of the closed double doors and thrust Grace's truck into Park. ''A lot of the radio stations in the rural areas only update their news and weather forecasts every twenty-four hours. Everyone knows they're not necessarily up-to-date. Everyone knows to check with the highway patrol or the national weather bureau for up-to-date information."

"Well, this is my first field trip out in the wilds of Virginia," Grace retorted indignantly, "and I didn't know."

"Obviously," Ryan said dryly as he slammed out of the still-running truck and pulled open the barn doors. It was still going to be hard as heck keeping them all safe while still doing his job, if trouble erupted across the valley as predicted. He didn't want to think about anyone getting hurt because he had failed to provide proper reconnaissance.

"Are you planning to be this judgmental and sarcastic the entire time we're in residence here?" she demanded as he jumped back in the snow-covered truck and pulled it all the way into the barn.

If it helps keep me from kissing you again? he thought, all too aware he had yet to forget the way her lips had softened beneath his and her body had melted against his. All too aware he wanted nothing more than to haul her into his arms and kiss her again—and probably would've done just that, had they not been here, and he in the middle of a case that was about to explode—he said, "What can I say?" He cut the motor on her truck, and they both alighted. "I'm a moody guy."

The prickliness required by his cover aside, however, he would do whatever necessary to keep her—and her students—safe. And that, in turn, meant not getting diverted by any romantic interludes with this oh-so-sexy schoolteacher. "Why?" he continued as she strode up beside him. As she squared off with him, her eyes flashed with temper. Unable to help himself, he taunted, "Is it going to be a problem if I am?"

Grace angled her chin up at him defiantly. "What do you think, Mr. McCoy?"

Ryan sighed as he studied the twin spots of color in her pretty cheeks, and the urge to kiss her again built to a fever pitch. His timing always had been the pits.

Behind them a door opened and slammed. Several sets of footsteps pounded across the porch.

"Ms. Tennessen, come quick!" one of the girls yelled in a high, anxious voice that sent Grace and Ryan both running in their direction. "Polly's sneezing and she can't stop!"

"IT'S THE DUST," Grace pronounced as she knelt over Polly, who was still sneezing intermittently. Her expression both commiserating and gentle, she fished a neatly pressed and folded handkerchief out of her handbag. "Here, put this hankie over your mouth and nose." Straightening, she looked at Ryan and said as if she had every right to order him around, "I'm going to need her antihistamine. The first-aid kit is in the center console of the truck."

He paused in the act of taking off his down jacket. Teacher in charge or not, he did not like the fact she was suddenly commandeering his home—and him— one bit. He was going to have to be firm with her if he did not want her to take over completely. "I suppose that means you want me to fetch it for you?"

"As well as all our luggage. Unless you'd rather stay here and help us clean." Grace regarded him coolly. Polly sneezed. Grace turned back to her charges. She surveyed the cluttered area, then began barking out orders right and left. He watched as she tossed a stack of old newspapers he hadn't yet had time to read into the trash.

"Now wait just a minute—" he said, as the bevy of serious little girls made quick work of organizing the mess he had worked six months to create.

"What did you say?" Grace asked as she strode into the kitchen. She looked around briefly, then spying the pantry, opened the door and dragged a vacuum cleaner, bucket and mop out into the middle of the floor.

"I think you ought to slow down."

"We have to get rid of the dust or Polly's going to become ill, and there's only one way to do that. Clean." Grace said as she pulled out an unopened bottle of pine disinfectant from under the kitchen sink and squirted some in the bucket. "In the meantime," she said as she added hot tap water to the strong-smelling liquid. "We also need something for dinner. What would you like us to cook for you?"

Ryan had underestimated her. Worse, much as he hated to admit it, what she was saying made sense. He rolled his eyes. "Whatever."

"No requests?"

"None I can repeat," he said through clenched teeth as he unwillingly appraised the woman.

She scowled at him as she removed her blazer and slipped it over the back of a chair. "You're really going to have to work on that attitude, Mr. McCoy."

Ryan tore his glance from the tempting curves of her breasts beneath the starched white fabric of her blouse. "Ms. Tennessen?" he said softly, looking deep into her jade green eyes.

"Yes, Mr. McCoy?"

Ryan leaned very close to her and lifted an errant golden tendril that had escaped the increasingly untidy blond topknot on her head. It felt like silk beneath his fingertips. "Just so you know," he whispered in her ear, "as far as I'm concerned, the sooner you're out of here, the better."

BY THE TIME Ryan had carted in the first aid kit, a cooler filled with juice and nutritious snacks, eight duffel bags crammed with gear and eight more back-packs crammed with books, Grace and the girls had tidied, vacuumed and dusted the downstairs. Polly's antihistamine was working, and Grace was ready to begin discussing the rest of the arrangements.

"Where would you like the girls and I to sleep to-night?" Grace asked Ryan as he took off his coat, stomped the snow off his boots and brushed the snow from his hair.

Ryan didn't want to think about what kind of night-gown Grace wore, never mind fantasize the way she would look in it. It was hard enough having her here, bringing order to his surroundings and filling the place with her feminine, feisty presence. "You can have the entire second floor," Ryan told her gruffly as he hung his coat on the hook by the door. He slanted a glance at the snow coming down steadily. "While you're here, I'll take the sofa downstairs."

"That's very generous of you."

He shrugged off her praise and instead concentrated on the wonderful aroma coming from the pots bubbling on the stove. What was she cooking that smelled so darn good? Nothing he ever fixed for himself smelled that way.

"Find what you needed for dinner?" he asked casually. Fortunately, just last week he had trucked in a two-month supply of food. He didn't know how long it would last for two adults and seven children, but they'd have plenty until the blizzard passed.

She sneaked a peek at whatever it was she'd just put in the oven, then turned to face him. "We're having pasta. I hope you don't mind eating dinner rather early. The girls generally dine around five-thirty."

"Sounds fine," Ryan said, working to put some twang into his voice.

Grace smiled at him officiously. "Good. It'll be ready shortly."

To Grace's chagrin, no sooner had everyone filled their plates and started to eat, than the questions began with all the girls talking at once.

"So are you from around here?"

"Where does your family live?"

"Do you have any brothers or sisters?"

"Do your mom and dad travel a lot, like ours do?"

"Girls!" Grace said, as she added dressing to her salad. "Mr. McCoy may not want to answer all those questions."

"I don't mind," Ryan said as he lavishly buttered a fluffy biscuit. He looked at the girls kindly. "I come from a large family in Georgia. I have six brothers, and they're all older than me. My dad is a building contractor who specializes in remodeling work, and my mom is a housewife, and they don't really travel much except on vacation."

"How'd you end up in Virginia?" Grace asked.

Ryan forked up a generous bite of spaghetti. "Fate, I guess. It just seemed a good place to do what had to be done."

Was it her imagination, Grace wondered, or was he imbuing his words with a double meaning she couldn't begin to understand? "Which was what?" she prodded curiously as she studied his handsome face.

Ryan turned his glance to the snowstorm, still raging with ever-growing intensity outside. "Follow my muse. Write some songs." He turned back to her and let his golden-brown eyes laser in on hers in the same penetrating way. "Get better at my chosen profession."

Grace swallowed around the sudden dryness in her throat. "And have you?"

Ryan shook his head wistfully. "I like to think I'm making progress, although there's still a lot I want and need to accomplish."

"How many songs have you written?" Darlene asked.

"Oh, lots," Ryan confided. "The problem is I haven't finished too many of them. But I'm working on that, too."

"Do you ever play in arenas or anything?" Hannah asked.

"No, but I did take my demo record down to the local radio stations and ask them to play it."

"And did they?" Clara asked breathlessly as she perched on the edge of her seat.

"No." Briefly, Ryan looked crestfallen and wounded to the core. "They advised me to wait until I was a little better at my craft."

"Oh!" the girls sympathetically cried out in unison.

"That's so mean!"

"Yeah, it's awful!"

"It's okay. All the great songwriters have to struggle." Ryan was quick to reassure them with a cocky attitude and confident grin. "I'll meet my goals here someday." His gaze drifted to Grace and moved slowly, sensually over her face. "Maybe sooner than any of us think."

The girls breathed a sigh of relief as Grace studied Ryan over the rim of her water glass. He seemed awfully cheerful about failing at his life's dream. Too cheerful, she thought. "I knew some musicians, writers and artists in college," she announced casually. "The single hardest thing any of them ever had to deal with was rejection. In fact most of them found it quite devastating and depressing. But you seem to take it in stride.''

"Well, you know what they say. The harder you have to work to make something happen, the sweeter the victory.''

Grace knew it took a lot of hope, determination and sheer perseverance to succeed in any of the arts, but she was suspicious. "Still, constant adversity can dampen even the strongest spirits.''

"When the going gets rough, as it often does, I just keep my end goal in mind. The sheer challenge of it all keeps me going.''

"I see.'' Maybe he was really talented. Maybe he needed to come all the way up to an isolated farmhouse on a mountaintop to find his muse—and finally succeed. So why then, Grace wondered, did she still have her doubts that was all he was up to?

"I would think you, a teacher, would appreciate a positive attitude in a person,'' Ryan continued, looking visibly aggrieved.

"Oh, I do,'' Grace murmured her agreement. It was just that she had a feeling Ryan McCoy was constantly leaving out a heck of a lot more than he was telling them. And she didn't like that.

YAWNING SLEEPILY, Letticia moved the curtain aside and looked out into the eerie whiteness of the January evening. "Look how h-h-hard the snow is coming d-d-down now,'' she murmured in wonderment. "You can't even s-s-see two feet in f-front of you.''

All the other girls crowded in beside Letticia. Hannah pointed to the front porch. "And look, it's drifting up against the front door and the windows, too. Can you believe it? It's almost up to the sill."

"Cool," Clara said. "Maybe we'll get stuck inside here forever!"

Brianna started in alarm. "That's not really going to happen, is it?" she demanded, her lower lip trembling.

"No, of course not." Grace knelt to give Brianna a reassuring hug.

"Clara had a point, though. What happens if the snow gets piled up against the door so high we can't get out?" Polly asked curiously, as Brianna began to furiously suck her thumb.

Greta rolled her eyes impatiently. "We'd climb out a window, dummy."

Brianna's eyes welled with tears. She still looked very worried.

Ryan knelt in front of her. "Would it make you feel better if I shoveled off the front porch right now?" Brianna nodded solemnly but did not stop sucking her thumb. "Okay, I'll go do that," Ryan said. He patted her shoulder reassuringly, then stood.

Grace reached for her boots. Knowing it wasn't fair to send him out there alone, she offered to help.

Because there was no way they could get out the front door, without causing an avalanche of snow inside the house, Ryan and Grace slipped out the back door. "Has Letticia always stuttered?" he asked.

Grace nodded. "She's working with a speech therapist back at school. It's going to take a while, but we think that as her self-esteem improves, so will her speech."

"It's good you're on top of the situation," he murmured. "What's with Brianna?" Ryan asked as they trudged through the snow piling up on the ground.

"That, I'm not so certain about." Grace ducked her head against the blowing, stinging snow as Ryan put a hand on her back and guided her around the side of the house. "She's just recently come to us."

His glance narrowed in concern. "Is she afraid of everything?"

"Pretty much." Grace tightened her scarf around her neck. "She's also painfully shy and new to boarding school in general."

"She cries a lot, I guess," Ryan supposed as he picked up a snow shovel leaning up against the side of the house and handed it to her.

Grace nodded, tightly gripping the handle in both gloved hands. Her back to the swirling snow, she looked up into the ruggedly handsome lines of his face. There were moments when she didn't have a clue what was going on with him, others when he was so kind and gentle he took her breath away. "Though I'm hoping that will pass when she gets adjusted to attending boarding school and becomes better friends with all the girls."

"Is it possible she's just homesick?" Ryan picked up what looked like a regular garden shovel for himself and, taking her elbow, guided her in the direction of the front porch.

"I wish that were the case, but her mother and father said she's been a 'nervous child' for quite a while now.''

Ryan regarded her with eyes that seemed to miss nothing. ''But they offered no explanation for her anxiety?''

Grace paused and bit down on her lower lip. ''I don't think they know. To tell you the truth, I also don't think they've spent a lot of time with her. They're both pilots in the military and they're often called out on assignment. In the past when that's happened, Brianna's been shuffled from one relative or friend to another, and it's left her feeling unsettled. Her parents hoped putting her in boarding school year-round would give more stability to her life.''

Ryan caught her hand and stopped her where they were, at the end of the sidewalk that led from the driveway to the front porch. ''They haven't considered resigning their commissions to be able to parent her on a full-time basis?''

''No.''

''And you don't think any less of them for that?'' Ryan said, frowning as he studied her upturned face.

Grace watched him stick his shovel into a good seven inches of snow and begin to scoop it up. ''It's not my place to judge, nor is it yours. Brianna's parents are doing what they feel they've been put here on earth to do. My role is to support them, educate Brianna and at the same time try to bring them together and make everyone happy.''

''That's quite a task,'' Ryan commented as he shoveled a path up the front steps to the porch of the farm-house.

Grace shrugged. It wasn't as hard for her to do that as he thought. Acutely aware of the little faces pressed up against the farmhouse windows watching them, she began shoveling, too. "My parents are both surgeons in the military. They've always been away a lot, too. Right now they're both stationed in Germany."

"So you were separated from them, growing up, I take it?" Ryan prodded curiously, finishing his side of the sidewalk quickly, then doubling back to help her with hers.

"And sometimes my folks were separated from each other, too," Grace said, as she worked on clearing the snow away from the front door. "So from sixth grade on, I was in boarding school, too."

"What about the rest of your students?" Ryan asked, still shoveling twice as much snow as she in half the time.

Grace hitched in a breath, aware her face was beginning to sting from the biting cold but also that she wouldn't trade these few moments alone with Ryan McCoy for anything. "Most of the girls at The Peach Blossom Academy are military brats, just like me, though an increasing number of them also have parents in the diplomatic corps." The sidewalk cleared, she helped shovel drifting snow off the steps, then followed him up onto the porch, where the drifts were much higher.

"We're on a year-round schedule with three-week breaks at the end of every quarter. Most of the girls go off to visit friends or family during their breaks, but if they can't, they're left at the school. Whenever possible, I try to take those who're left behind on field trips—or little vacations—so they don't feel left out or cheated.'' The way she often had, when she'd been left behind and had nowhere to go. ''That's why I have girls from age six to fourteen in my group.''

He paused a moment to look down into her face. ''That's quite a commitment to your students.''

''I enjoy it,'' Grace said, surprised to find how incredibly elated his words of praise made her feel. ''They're like family to me.''

''So I'm beginning to notice,'' he said softly, admiration shining in his eyes.

Their smiles meshed a moment longer. Embarrassed, and far too aware of him, Grace was the first to turn away.

As they cleared the last of the piles of snow away from the windows and doors, the girls clapped and cheered inside. Grace paused to smile and raise one gloved hand in the victory sign. Beside her, Ryan grinned and mugged for the girls, who predictably went crazy and cheered all the louder.

''Seems like we made them happy,'' Ryan remarked.

Yes, they had, Grace thought.

''And you, Mr. McCoy, have a heart underneath all that bluster,'' Grace teased back impulsively.

''That's not surprising.'' Ryan took her shovel and carried it for her as he helped her off the front porch. Together they circled around back to clear off those steps, too. "I am a songwriter, after all." He flashed her an easy grin. "I'm supposed to be all heart."

"WHEN ARE YOU GOING to sing one of your songs for us, Mr. McCoy?" the girls asked an hour later, as they sat around the farmhouse living room in their flannel pajamas and matching peach-and-white-plaid robes.

Ryan finished stoking the fire and replaced the mesh screen. Avoiding Grace's glance, he ducked his head in an aw-shucks manner completely at odds with his overly confident personality. "That's right nice of you little ladies to ask, but—"

"Oh, please, please, please!" the girls clamored.

"I'm not all that good yet," Ryan protested, for the first time beginning to look a little flustered, and embarrassed, too.

"I'm sure you're much better than you give yourself credit for," Grace interjected. Ryan McCoy was a very intelligent man. If he'd put the rest of his life on hold and moved into this farmhouse to begin a songwriting career, then he had done so knowing he would make a success of it.

"And we really, really want to hear you sing," the girls all agreed.

Grace had to admit she was burning with curiosity. "And I would, too." She just hoped he wouldn't sing them a particularly sad ballad, because she was a sucker for an emotional song and could get tears in her eyes quicker than she could draw a breath.

"All right." Ryan sighed as he got up to retrieve his guitar. "I'll sing one I've been working on recently, but I warn all of you, it's not finished, not nearly.''

"That's okay," the girls decided promptly. And Grace knew then and there that all her students were totally in love with him, groupies in the making....

Ryan picked up his guitar and settled it across his lap. He fiddled a bit with the strings, tuning it—rather badly, Grace noted, surprised, then strummed a few chords and burst into song:

"Well, my gal she done drove off in the pickup truck
One fine and wintry day.
I said, 'Gal, why not come back to see me?'
And instead she said, 'Eat my dust'.''

Ryan put down his guitar. He breathed a huge sigh of relief. "Well, that's all so far. What do you think?" he asked anxiously.

It was clear from the looks on their faces, the girls didn't know what to say. Grace didn't, either. She loved country music with the same passion she loved Mozart, but—there was no getting around it—Ryan was no Garth Brooks or George Strait. Nor, judging from the quality of his singing voice, was he ever likely to be.

"The melody sounded familiar," Hannah, always the bravest, ventured finally.

"Did it?" Ryan wrinkled his brow and looked confused. "You know, to tell you the truth, I kinda thought so, too.''

"But it was pretty," one of the girls was quick to praise.

"Thanks." Ryan repeated his aw-shucks grin.

Her own emotions in turmoil, Grace stood and offered an efficient smile of her own. "Say good-night to Mr. McCoy, girls."

"'Night, Ryan!" they all shouted.

Grace shepherded them upstairs to the makeshift beds she had prepared for them, using Ryan's blankets and sheets. She made sure they were settled for the night, then returned to the first floor. As she entered the room, Ryan was still sitting on the sofa in front of the fire, the guitar on his lap. His golden-brown hair was soft and shiny, the long layers gently mussed. The hint of evening beard was on his face, and the faint scent of soap and aftershave clung to his jaw.

He looked at her curiously, his golden-brown eyes glimmering with—was that *mischief?* "You didn't say what you thought of my singing," he said eventually.

Grace didn't know what he was up to, she only knew he was playing with her. Grace forced her lips into a parody of a smile and continued to regard him bluntly. "You really want my opinion?" she asked sweetly.

For a moment he went very still, then he shrugged and put his guitar aside. "Yeah, I do," he said softly as he patted the sofa cushion beside him.

Grace ignored his invitation to sit, moved to the mantel instead and stood with her back to the fire. She folded her arms in front of her. "The reason your melody sounded familiar to the girls is the tune you—

shall we say borrowed—was 'Oh, Susannah'." She hummed a few bars to illustrate her point, using first the standard lyrics, then the ones he had written.

"Well, how about that." Ryan slapped his denim-clad knee. "I never would've figured that out."

That, Grace did not believe for one second. "Furthermore, your guitar is hideously out of tune," she continued.

Ryan blinked. "How can you tell?" he asked innocently.

"Because I have an ear that is not made of tin. Furthermore," Grace continued, completely without pity, "you're a terrible vocalist. I'd wager you could not carry a tune if your life depended on it. And, I have the feeling that none of this is news to you. You not only know you're terrible, you get off on demonstrating that fact to your audience, and then watching them squirm as they try not to hurt your feelings."

Ryan rolled to his feet. His jaw was rigid as he emitted a lengthy sigh of regret. "Well, you sure didn't fall into that trap now, did you?" he recapped so softly she had to strain to hear.

"The question is," Grace went on, as if he hadn't spoken, even as he took another step near, "why are you doing all this? Despite all the 'shucks' and 'ma'ams' and 'how-de-dos' you've been uttering tonight, I know you're not dumb. Far from it, as a matter of fact."

Several seconds ticked by as he stared at her in mounting disbelief. Although his stance was easy, she detected an intensity beneath that indolence that made her wary. "So what's your point?" he asked softly, pleasantly.

Grace ignored the faint tightening at the corners of his lips and the glimmer of anger in his golden-brown eyes. "The point is, you—Mr. Ryan McCoy—are putting on one of the most elaborate charades I have ever seen in my life."

"Now hold on one red-hot minute—" he protested heatedly, abruptly beginning to lose his temper, too.

"Which in turn makes me wonder," Grace said, taking matters into her own hands and closing the distance between them completely. She was going to get the truth from this country Romeo if it killed her! She tilted her head up to his and, ignoring the need for caution, pressed on, determined to end this coy deception of his once and for all. "Who are you, Ryan McCoy?" she demanded impatiently. "And what are you really doing here?"

Chapter Four

Ryan had known Grace Tennessen was going to disrupt his life from the get-go, but he sure hadn't figured on this! "I don't have the foggiest idea what you're talking about," Ryan declared, determined not to let her unmask him.

Grace glared at him. "Don't you?"

Ryan squeezed his eyes shut in frustration. When he opened them again, he spoke with infinite patience. "No."

Grace planted both hands on her slender hips. "I can spot a phony, Ryan. I have certainly met and dated enough of them over the years."

The thought of Grace with other men was a curiously unwelcome one. Ryan pushed aside his unprecedented possessiveness where a woman was concerned, and concentrated instead on goading her onto another subject. "Is that what turned you into the ice princess you are today?"

Color bloomed in her pretty cheeks. "What made me swear off romance is none of your business," she said tightly.

Ryan touched a few untidy silken tendrils that had escaped the knot of golden hair on the back of her head. He wondered how long her hair actually was, and what it would look like down. "I beg to differ, princess. Anything that makes you accuse me of all sorts of wild things is very much my business."

Grace flushed and pulled away, the pained expression on her face telling him he'd hit his target. "You're just upset because I'm on to you," she accused, as she lifted a hand to her hair.

Ryan knew that was true. More damning still, he had the feeling Grace could see through him as no one ever had, and that was definitely not good. Her curiosity could put her and the girls in grave danger.

Finished tidying her hair, she demanded, "So, are you going to tell me what you're up to, or not?"

Her determination to unmask him was so fierce, her will so strong, he had no choice but to take drastic measures and scare her away. "I'll do better than that," Ryan said softly, tugging Grace into his embrace and clamping an iron arm around her waist. "I'll show you."

For the second time that day, he lowered his head to hers, cupped the back of her neck with the palm of his hand and angled his lips over hers. It all happened so fast Grace barely had time to widen her eyes and gasp before he pressed his lips to hers and delivered a sensual, searing kiss. As Ryan had figured, it didn't take long at all for her lips to part or her body to soften seductively and melt against his. What surprised him was the way the heat within him altered states, from the cool logical path of a job-related seduction, meant to shock and frighten her into curtailing her meddlesome curiosity and staying away, to the more primal, less controlled, states of wanting and need.

And want her, he did. He'd never kissed lips so giving and gentle or—yes, there was no other word for it, innocent. Never felt a woman so athletically fit or sensual or whose skin was so soft and fragile, like the finest silk. She smelled of flowers and woman. And as far as his need, well… Reluctantly, he acknowledged that, too.

Neither emotion was anything he could afford. For all their sakes and safety he ended the kiss, and as he did, Grace apparently came to her senses. She slapped him across the face. "You had no right to do that!" she said, fuming, her jade green eyes glittering furiously.

Ryan rubbed his stinging skin, knowing he deserved a lot worse for letting himself get even this involved with a woman who should have been—who was—nothing more than an encumbrance to getting his job done. After all, it wasn't just *their* well-being at stake, but many others. And it was up to him to garner enough evidence to prevent a violent attack and facilitate arrests.

"I agree," he said gruffly, as irked with his own lack of control as he was with her astonished reaction to it. "There's nothing worse than two people, trapped together by circumstance, getting involved, just 'cause they were bored and lonely," he told her, glaring down at her. He had done that before, to poor result.

He damn sure wasn't going to fall into the same trap again!

"I assure you," Grace stormed hotly as she rubbed the moisture from their kiss off her lips, "I am not bored and I am not lonely!"

"Good," Ryan replied just as contentiously. "Neither am I. So we shouldn't have any problems being tempted while we wait for this snowstorm to pass and the roads to clear."

Grace stared at him. "Are you saying you won't kiss me again?"

With regret and a great burst of conscience, he nodded. "Princess, that's a promise. If we kiss again, and I say if, it's going to be because you kissed me, not the other way around!"

Grace rolled her eyes and exhaled contempt. Her breasts rose and fell in agitation with every breath she took. "That'll be the day!"

"I agree," Ryan said smoothly, hoping that would indeed stay the case. "Therefore, the two of us should be safe from making any more foolish mistakes, shouldn't we?"

Her chin jutting forward, Grace continued to glare at him. "Back to this 'singing' business. I still want to know what you're trying to pull here."

Ryan frowned. He had hoped she'd given up on this. He quirked a brow. "I don't owe you any explanations, princess."

She flashed him a smile that did not reach her eyes. "Humor me, anyway."

"Whether you agree or not doesn't matter to me,"

Ryan was able to say quite honestly. "I believe I'm quite talented in my field." *It just doesn't happen to be music,* he amended silently. "Now," he said, regarding her with a playful look that encompassed her from the top of her beautiful head to the tips of her dainty little toes, "if you don't want to be tempted to kiss me again, I think you'd better head on upstairs and go to bed."

Ryan could see she did not like being ordered around, but she clearly liked the possibility of another sensual tangle even less.

Grace speared him with a defiantly haughty look. "I'll go, but only because I'm exhausted and it's been a very difficult day."

Ryan figured as much but it didn't matter. The important thing was putting—and then maintaining—a lot more distance between them.

HER LIPS AND BODY still tingling from Ryan's extemporaneous embrace and fiery kiss, Grace went upstairs and checked on the girls. Exhausted from the tumultuous events of the day, they had arranged themselves in the two spare bedrooms. Snuggled in their Academy sleeping bags, which were lined up across the floor, all were sleeping soundly.

She walked across the hall to the master bedroom, which contained the only bed in the rambling two-story farmhouse. Ryan had graciously given it to her, but now, after the two heated kisses, plus his continued refusal to be honest with her, she was not sure she wanted to sleep in the cozy-looking double bed where he usually slept.

Knowing, however, she had little choice if she didn't want to be answering a lot of questions from the girls—and she didn't!—she went into the adjacent bath, peeled off her clothes and put on a pair of flannel pajamas in the same peach, beige and cream plaid the girls were wearing. She took down her hair, brushed it thoroughly, washed her face, slathered on moisturizer and brushed her teeth.

Finished, she left the hall door open, so she'd wake promptly if any of the girls woke during the night and needed her, then went back into Ryan's bedroom, switched off the light and climbed into the cozy-looking bed with the homemade quilts and worn, mismatched sheets. To her consternation, the bed was scented with the fragrance of Ryan's cologne and the clean, masculine scent of his skin and hair.

She groaned softly, knowing that was all she needed—to feel enveloped in his sensual presence for the entire night. But try as she might, she could not get him off her mind. And it wasn't because he was one of the most ruggedly handsome men she had ever met. Or because her every feminine instinct told her he wasn't telling her everything that was going on there. Or even that he kissed her with a thoroughness and sensuality and tenderness she had only dreamed about.

It was because of the way he made her feel, like she was completely, gloriously alive in a way she had never been, even when she'd been engaged to be married. And wise or not, she wasn't sure she wanted to let that feeling go.

"Mr. McCoy."

Ryan groaned at the soft melodious sound of Grace Tennessen's voice whispering from somewhere above him, but did not open his eyes. "Stop calling me that," he ordered grumpily as he snatched the pillow and put it over his head.

"Okay," Grace said with a sweetly voiced patience that made him grit his teeth all the more, "*Ryan.* I need you to get up now."

Ryan opened one eye and focused on the mantel. The clock said it wasn't even 6:00 a.m. Having spent most of the night tossing and turning on the battered old couch thinking about the hot, sensual kisses he and Grace had shared, knowing that because it was *still* snowing outside, there was likely to be no criminal activity on Blue Mountain, or anywhere else in the vicinity, he was not inclined to rise and shine at the crack of dawn just because Miss Prim and Proper thought they should. He groaned again and propped his forearm across his brow. He could only hope she didn't look as pretty first thing in the morning as she had last night. "Why?" he finally asked.

"Because I need you to get up and put on your clothes before the girls wake up," Grace told him haughtily.

Ryan groaned again and rubbed his eyes. He had no problem with what she was requesting. In fact, it made sense for him to pull on at least a T-shirt and jeans. He did have a problem with the demanding, autocratic tone she was using on him, and he wasn't about to let her get away with it.

"I wouldn't want them to see anything…well, indecent," she said nervously, wringing her hands.

Ryan flung the blanket away from his chest, swung his bare legs over the edge of the sofa and vaulted ever so deliberately to his feet. "Like this?" he said.

Grace gaped at the sight of Ryan McCoy. Though it shouldn't have made any difference, he seemed even more powerfully built nearly naked, than when clothed. A telltale warmth stealing through her, she noted all six feet five inches of him was solidly muscled and covered with touchably smooth, golden skin. A mat of thick, whorling golden-brown hair covered his chest and arrowed down into a pair of electric blue briefs that left little about either his burgeoning desire or his anatomy to the imagination. Oh, she thought as her throat suddenly became as dry as the Sahara, the man was well-endowed.

"Well, don't just stand there," he intoned dryly as she shivered under the blatant sexual intent in his gaze. "Hand me my jeans." He grinned, as if at some private joke that only he understood. "Unless you *want* me to stand here until you look your fill?"

Grace swallowed hard, her desire for him as evident as his for her. Blushing fiercely and wishing she could do something about the way her nipples were beading beneath her lacy bra and clinging pink cashmere turtleneck, she spun away from him. "You're incorrigible," she fumed.

"So I've been told," Ryan agreed lazily as she snatched up his jeans and flung them at him with hands that trembled slightly. "The T-shirt and flannel shirt, too," he ordered, mocking her earlier commanding attitude.

With a beleaguered sigh, she blindly handed him both over her shoulder.

Their hands brushed as he took them from her.

"You can look now," he said drolly, as he tugged the long-sleeved T-shirt over his head and shoved his hands through the sleeves.

Arms folded in front of her, she spun around, colored again when she noticed he'd yet to even put on his flannel shirt and his fly was still unzipped. "Honestly!" she exclaimed with a toss of her head, vacating the room abruptly.

"What's the matter?" Ryan said as he followed her into the kitchen, shrugging on his shirt. "Never seen a man get dressed before?"

"As a matter of fact—" She tore her eyes away from the way he was smoothing the soft cotton jersey over his washboard-flat abs and tucking his shirt over that into the waistband of his jeans.

"What?" Ryan said as she continued to react as if he was standing in front of her buck naked.

Grace shot another tentative look at him and then blushed a fiery pink as he routinely buttoned his jeans at the waist. "Nothing," she said in an even more strangled tone, still feeling unaccountably shocked and unaccountably nervous about what she'd seen. *What would it be like to make love with him?*

Ryan paused, his hand on the metal tab of his open zipper. "Either you're toying with me," he said slowly, as he closed his zipper with a soft metal swish. "Or..." All buttoned and zipped, he let his hand fall idly to his side and kept his eyes on her face.

"Or what?" she prodded, wetting her lips and drawing another caution-filled breath.

"Or you have never seen a naked man before," he said softly, grinning. "Or even anything close."

Blushing, Grace scoffed in exasperation as he slowly closed the distance between them. "Of course I have."

"Really." His sensually curved lips tilted up at the corners as a thousand fantasies filled her head. "When?"

She shrugged vaguely, loath to admit how close to the truth he was. "Movies."

Ryan leaned toward her and qualified bluntly, "I meant *in person*."

"Must you be so annoying this early in the morning?" she demanded, tearing her eyes from the direction of his fly.

"Hey." Ryan thumped his chest and willed the blood to leave his groin—immediately. "I'm not the one who woke you up. You woke me."

Grace tossed her head and smoothed her hands over the lines of her impeccably tailored white wool trousers. "Only because I had to do so."

Ryan tore his eyes from her trim waist, enticing hips and long, lissome thighs and with a great deal of difficulty, returned it to her eyes. "You didn't answer my question."

Grace shrugged in an unconcerned manner and leaned against the counter. "That's because we've digressed so much I've forgotten what it was."

Now that, Ryan thought as he watched her lower lip tremble and her jade green eyes widen, was an outright lie. He closed the distance between them until it was possible to feel the warmth of her body and inhale the soft flowery scent that clung to her hair and skin.

"Is it possible?" he asked softly, dropping his voice another insinuating notch and clamping a hand on either side of her. With her caged in front of him, he let his glance roam over her upturned face. "Is your primness and innocence *not* an act meant to put me in my place?"

Grace stiffened and jerked in a shallow breath. She regarded him with a haughty stare that would have decimated a lesser man. "I'm sure I don't know what you're talking about," she said icily.

Liar, Ryan thought, as he leaned even closer. "Then I'll put it as plain as I know how to make it," he drawled. "Are you a virgin? 'Cause you're sure as heck acting like a virgin."

Face flaming, Grace planted a hand across his chest and shoved him aside. "That is none of your business," she told him haughtily as she strode past.

Ryan followed her to the walk-in pantry. "So you are a virgin."

Grace tossed her head and admonished briskly, "Mr. McCoy!"

He scowled as she searched the shelves. "You're doing it again," he reminded. Addressing him with a formality he did not like.

"So I am." She plucked a box of biscuit mix, a jar of peach jam and a canister of quick-cooking oats from the well-stocked shelves. "And I'll thank you not to talk like this around me."

Ryan moved back to let her pass, then grinned and rubbed a hand along his unshaven jaw. He didn't know why, but the thought she had yet to be with a man was a sobering one. He narrowed his eyes at her speculatively as he followed her over to the cupboards that contained the pots and pans. "And you're how old—?"

"Twenty-six, if you must know," she said dryly as she selected the biggest pot he had and a measuring cup and utensils from the drawer.

"Hmm."

Grace uttered a beleaguered sigh as she efficiently measured out water and salt into the big stainless steel pot. "You don't have to say it," she said as she switched on the burner to high and set the pot on top of it.

Unwilling to admit just how much he enjoyed having her in the farmhouse kitchen, or how much she had eased the loneliness of his present life with her sweet and feisty presence, Ryan studied the color flowing into her pretty cheeks. "I don't have to say what?" he asked curiously.

Grace met his eyes with a bravery that was both astonishing and touching. "That I'm the last twenty-six-year-old virgin on earth." Her lips curved in a rueful smile, and a hint of resignation crept into her jade green eyes before she lowered her thick, golden lashes and turned away. "I already know it."

"So how come?" Ryan watched her measure out biscuit mix and water. It couldn't possibly have been for lack of offers. A woman that gorgeous had to have men lined up for blocks who—unlike him—would've done anything she pleased to be a significant part of her life. No, if she privately lamented her lack of experience and yet had still said no, it had to have been for a good reason. "Is it because all the men you've dated have been jerks?"

"That's part of the reason," Grace conceded with a frown as she rolled up her sleeves and squished the mixture together with her hands.

"But not all?" he guessed, imagining a woman like Grace would need love and tenderness and commitment thrown into the mix before she gave herself to anyone.

Grace sighed wistfully as she patted a quarter cup of the soft, moist dough into a biscuit and laid it on a baking sheet. "No, not all."

Then what? Ryan wondered, as the phone began to ring and footsteps sounded on the floor above them.

Resenting the interruption, but knowing if he didn't answer it, they'd just call again and again, he picked up the phone. "Ryan McCoy here," he said gruffly.

"Ryan!" a familiar voice chirped in his ear. "It's

Mandy! I wondered how you were faring in all this snow!"

With effort, Ryan forced himself to be polite to the most-aggressive of the husband-hunting local women who were after him. "I'm fine, Mandy," he told her cheerfully, thinking, *Especially when I'm kissing Grace.*

"I'd love to come over and keep you company," Mandy lamented with a flirtatiousness that grated on Ryan's nerves like fingernails on a chalkboard, "but I can't get out of my driveway."

"Well, that's right pleasant of you, Mandy, but you don't have to worry about me any longer," Ryan said, shooting a look at Grace—who, he noted curiously, was beginning to look a little piqued. "My woman's here. She—Grace—got in just before the snowstorm hit."

As Ryan had hoped, his announcement had the desired effect. There was a long silence, then a sigh. "You're kidding, right?" Mandy eventually asked glumly.

"Nope." Ryan grinned at Grace, glad her presence there had done this much for him. If he knew Mandy, she'd be on the phone all morning, spreading the word around.

"But after all this time—I mean, when she didn't show up at Christmas—" Mandy complained.

Ryan knew exactly what Mandy and everyone else had thought: that his fiancée didn't exist. Fortunately, Grace had stepped in to "prove" them all wrong. In that sense, her presence had been very helpful, and Ryan was grateful.

"Call Hindale if you don't believe me," Ryan continued, as Grace slapped biscuits onto the baking pan with a decisive thud, one after another. "He caught us smooching yesterday afternoon on his way back to town."

"Oh, well—" Mandy sighed, her disappointment in losing out to Grace obvious.

"You-all stay warm now, you hear?" Ryan said, as even more color crept into Grace's cheeks.

"Sure." Mandy sighed again. "You, too."

To Ryan's relief, Mandy severed the connection. He hung up, too.

"What was that all about" Grace inquired, pivoting sharply and looking deep into his eyes, before her lips took on a sardonic curl. "Or should I ask?"

Ryan watched Grace fiddle with the temperature dial for the oven. "That was Mandy—one of the women I was telling you about yesterday."

Grace slid the biscuit pan into the oven with more than necessary force. She slammed the oven door, wiped her hands on a dish towel. "Did she get the message?" Grace bit out, quirking her golden brows in his direction.

Ryan wondered what it was that had Grace so ticked off. After all, it wasn't as though he had anything going with Mandy or any of the other women around Blue Mountain Gap; he'd made that clear yesterday. "It appears so, yeah," Ryan answered. Furthermore, with any luck, Mandy would do what Hindale hadn't and spread the news that Ryan's fiancée was "visiting him" in no time flat. But Grace did not seem to appreciate his good fortune, Ryan noted, perplexed.

Was it possible?... Could it be?...

Ryan began to smile, but before he had a chance to figure out if Grace was jealous of Mandy or not, a shout came from upstairs, then another. Both shouts were swiftly followed by the sound of footsteps running down the hall, down the stairs. Seconds later, the farmhouse kitchen was filled with seven sleep-rumpled girls, all chattering at once.

"Miss Tennessen! Look at all the snow outside, will you?"

"Have you ever seen so much snow in your life?"

"I sure haven't, but then I've never been in a blizzard before."

"I wonder if it'll ever stop snowing!"

"There must be at least two to three feet of snow on the ground out there," Grace said, finishing the biscuits quickly and moving with the girls to the window.

"More, where it's drifted," Ryan said, joining them at the pane.

"But the snow seems to have finally slowed down a bit." Given the weather, he wondered how long Grace and her students would be there with him. He knew he should want to get rid of them right away, but for reasons he chose not to examine too closely he wasn't all that eager to see them go just yet.

Grace breathed a sigh of relief and looked like the time for them to leave couldn't come a moment too soon for her. "Thank heavens for small miracles," she murmured, meeting his eyes.

With effort, Ryan checked his own disappointment and kept a poker face. Whether Grace wanted to admit it or not, it had been a miracle they'd shown up here instead of the Hindale farm, so she and her girls had a safe, warm place to stay, and he didn't have to weather the storm alone.

"Can we check the television and see what the weather report says?" Letticia said, tugging on Ryan's sleeve.

"Sure," Ryan said, reluctantly tearing his eyes from Grace's relieved expression.

With the seven girls all chattering away a mile a minute, he led the way into the living room and switched on the television. And together they sat down in front of the set and heard the first and most dismal forecast of the day.

"At least we have electricity," Ryan told the girls when the forecast had ended. "Many people in West Virginia are without electricity, even as we speak."

And there were others that were missing—a runaway bride from Pennsylvania, a young mother and her baby from Maryland. No, Grace and the girls were lucky to be right where they were.

FIFTEEN MINUTES LATER, Grace had the coffee brewing, the orange juice made and the quick-cooking oats piping hot. She had just taken the biscuits from the oven when the girls came rushing back into the kitchen, Ryan in tow.

"It's not supposed to stop snowing until this afternoon!" the girls declared.

Grace directed everyone to sit at the table as Ryan informed, "They said it'll be days until the interstate highways are cleared."

Though her heart was pounding, Grace feigned nonchalance and avoided Ryan's probing gaze as she began dishing up oatmeal laced with chunks of apple, cinnamon and brown sugar. "I guess I'll have to call the school after breakfast and tell them we'll be stuck here a few more days. Maybe you girls should call your parents, too, if it's all right with Mr. McCoy."

Ryan poured them both a mug of steaming coffee and set one in front of her with a provoking grin. "It's fine with me. And as long as everyone is going to be here a while longer, I think everyone—including you, Miss Tennessen—" he emphasized in a silken voice that sent shivers down her spine "—should call me Ryan."

"Cool!" the girls hollered.

"It isn't the school policy to allow the girls to speak so familiarly with an adult," Grace said with a tight, offended smile, every bit as determined to keep the barriers up between them as he was to tear them down.

"Like a lot of things, it's just too familiar," Ryan taunted softly.

Grace didn't have to look into his eyes and see the heat sizzling there to know he was talking about their kiss, and the unconscionable way she had responded to it. "That's it exactly," Grace said, knowing that no matter what, she couldn't let herself be seduced into his arms again. His kisses were just too compelling.

"Miss Tennessen?" Polly asked around a sneeze.

"Are you blushing?" Greta demanded, shoving her glasses higher on the bridge of her nose.

"It looks like you're blushing," Hannah teased cheerfully, as she rocked backward in her chair.

"How come?" Clara asked, confused.

"I know why!" Darlene said, pointing to the health book she'd brought to the table with her.

"So do I," Ryan said, his voice overriding the girls' voices, as he lavishly slathered peach jam on both piping hot halves of a flaky, golden biscuit.

Grace felt her face turn all the warmer. "I am not blushing."

"Looks like you are to me," Ryan drawled in a cajoling voice as he lifted the biscuit to his lips.

Refusing to be seduced into yet another flirtation with the would-be singing star, Grace glowered at Ryan. He continued watching her with an expression of sheer pleasure.

One by one, the girls lit up. Noticing, it was all Grace could do not to groan in dismay. Now they were all sure there was something going on. Before anyone could comment on it further, however, breakfast was interrupted by the rat-a-tat sound of—Grace stopped eating her oatmeal abruptly, as did everyone else. Mirroring her students' startled looks, she looked at Ryan. "Is that...gunfire?"

"Sure sounds like it." Ryan shrugged amiably and continued eating as if it were no big deal.

A shiver of uneasiness slid down Grace's spine. Though she couldn't put her finger on it exactly, there was something she did not like or trust about Ryan's neighbor across the valley.

"It's probably just Hindale and some of his buddies having a little target practice," Ryan soothed.

Grace didn't want to think about bullets or guns anywhere near her charges. "In the snow?"

Ryan shrugged. "He practices almost every morning, no matter what the weather." Finished, he rose and carried his dishes to the sink. "It's nothing to worry about," he told her bluntly as he ran cool water over the sticky interior of the dish. "Just stay inside until it's over."

Grace was no fool, she had planned to do just that.

Throat dry, she watched him stride lazily to the coat rack by the back door. "Where are you going?"

"The snow's inspired me." He picked up a pad and pen off the counter and slid it into the pocket of his coat. "I think I'll go out and take a walk and see if I can't write some lyrics about this winter wonderland we've been blessed with."

Grace was about to protest that it was awfully cold—and quite possibly dangerous, given the recent spate of gunfire—for him to be doing that.

Before she could get a word out, Ryan gave Grace a droll look. "Although the girls here were quite appreciative of the effort I put into my music, some people think I haven't been working nearly hard enough on my songwriting craft."

Grace flushed at the thinly veiled complaint.

Maybe she had been a little too honest with him last night, but despite his fervent denials to the contrary, her inner radar for frauds still told her he was not what he was trying to seem. He was far too intelligent to think he had a chance of ever becoming a successful country-and-western singer-songwriter. And despite his lazy posturing, she couldn't see him doing anything he wasn't successful at for long.

"When will you be back?" she asked calmly, aware she was now standing close enough to see the shadow of beard on his face and to recall how rough and sexy it had felt brushing up against her skin as they had kissed.

He grinned and sauntered even closer. "Worried about me?"

No, of course not, she started to say, as her cheeks flushed with indignation. Then wary of the girls who were still listening avidly, she carefully crafted her answer so it would not reveal any of their attraction to each other, and would be suitable for the children's ears, yet absolutely truthful all the same. "I worry about everyone who has to venture out in this kind of weather," she told him cavalierly, willing the color in her cheeks to go away.

"That's nice to know." He lifted a hand to her cheek and touched it briefly. His glance settling on hers, he said, "Stay here and keep the girls inside till I get back."

Was that protectiveness she saw in his eyes?

"When will you be back?" Grace asked, albeit a

little throatily, surprised to discover she felt very discomfited by the thought of being without him.

"I don't know exactly." His eyes abruptly turned grim. "An hour or so. Maybe more."

Giving her no chance to ask anything else, Ryan slipped out the door and shut it softly behind him.

Chapter Five

Half an hour later, Ryan looked through the high-powered telescope as he talked to headquarters via the secured telephone line. "There are ten of them outside now," he reported to Juliet. "Nine males. One female. All seem to be dressed in some sort of combat fatigues. And get this—they've got a United States Army tank sitting just inside their barn door."

"It's not surprising. A tank was reported stolen a few weeks ago from an Army training ground near there. The two soldiers they think were involved in the theft have gone AWOL."

"Which means they could be with Hindale," Ryan surmised grimly.

"Probably, yeah."

Ryan watched as Hindale walked around, seemingly spouting off orders to his subordinates. He did not want to think about the danger Grace and the girls could be in, but there was no denying their lives were in jeopardy. The cache of weapons and ammunition in his sights was mind-boggling. They could hold off capture for days with their firepower. "It looks like they're gearing up for something."

On the other end of the line, Juliet concurred. "Our reconnaissance says they're going to hit their target in western Virginia as soon as the weather clears."

Ryan swore silently to himself. "You still think someone in the sheriff's department in town is involved in this, too?"

"Yes, so don't go calling on any of the local authorities for help if you do get in trouble."

Could this assignment get any more difficult?

Juliet paused. "How is their shooting?"

Ryan zoomed in a little closer as another round was fired and ten tin cans jumped in the air. "Judging by the targets, dead-on."

"What kind of weapons are they using for their target practice?" Juliet asked.

"Need you even ask? Automatic."

"Great."

"Tell me about it," Ryan said, and rubbed at the knot of tension gathering in the back of his neck. "I've got a schoolteacher and seven schoolkids from The Peach Blossom Academy for Young Women staying at my place."

There was a long silence. Finally Juliet croaked, "You're kidding, right?"

I wish. Briefly Ryan explained how Grace and the girls had come to stay with him for the duration of the blizzard. "I'd like to get them out of here today—"

Still sounding appalled, Juliet interrupted, "There's

nothing you can do, with the roads as bad as they are. The whole state of Virginia has closed down.''

Ryan had figured as much when he'd first walked out on the hard-packed snow. The streets were going to be hell to clear. Nevertheless, he had a job to do, and the first order of business was moving Grace and the girls out of harm's way. ''How long before they get the roads open again?'' he asked briskly.

''Optimistically? Several days.''

Ryan groaned. ''I've got to get Grace and the kids out of here before anything does go down.'' The question, Ryan conceded privately, was how. Even assuming the snow would stop long enough to allow the bureau to bring a helicopter in to airlift them out, doing so would garner too much attention. And attention was the one thing he did not need from Hindale and his bullet-happy cronies.

''Hey,'' Juliet prodded, after another long thoughtful pause. ''You're not falling for this woman, are you?''

Was he? Ryan wondered. There were sparks between them, no doubt about that. They had only to come face-to-face with each other or try to have a conversation and the air between them was lit with enough electricity to fuel a furnace on the coldest winter day. But as for the rest, Grace was innocent. His job with the Bureau had made him cynical to a fault. Sexually and otherwise, she was pure as the driven snow outside. He was accustomed to doing what he had to do to get the job done, and as he was most often involved in undercover work, that meant faking a helluva lot.

But there had been no faking his response to her lips. When they'd kissed, when she'd wreathed her arms around his neck and molded her soft body next to his, the rest of the world had faded away. For those few moments there had been only the two of them, the desire running like a river between them, and the connection they'd made binding them as they kissed and kissed and kissed. He sometimes worried he'd worked undercover for so long he'd forgotten how to connect with people, one-on-one. Being with Grace made him feel it was still going to be possible for him to do that. Being with Grace made him *want* to do that.

"You won't be able to do your best to protect Grace and those kids unless you are not emotionally involved with them," Juliet continued sternly.

"I'm aware of that," Ryan retorted gruffly, grimacing at even the thought that he was behaving in an unprofessional manner.

"Then I don't have to tell you to keep your distance—emotionally speaking."

"No one has to tell me how to do my job," Ryan grumbled back. The problem was, staying away from Grace was easier said than done.

"YOU'RE REALLY WORRIED about Ryan, aren't you?" Polly asked as she stifled another sneeze.

"You know how artists are," Grace fibbed, as she wiped down the counters and kitchen table with a warm, sudsy dishrag. "They often lose track of time. I wouldn't want Ryan to get so caught up in his song-writing that he ends up with frostbite."

Brianna followed Grace around as she finished tidy-ing up the kitchen, sucking her thumb furiously all the while. Finally she took her thumb out of her mouth long enough to spear Grace with a look and say, "He's not a very good singer."

Out of the mouths of babes, Grace thought wryly as she knelt before the shy seven-year-old. "What makes you say that?"

"'Cause he isn't," Greta stated seriously, pushing her glasses up on the bridge of her nose while Letticia cuddled against her sleepily, rubbing her eyes.

"I just wonder if he knows that," Hannah said, as she paced the kitchen restlessly, looking out the win-dow at the sparsely falling snow and frosty gray sky.

"You'd think he would have to know," Darlene sighed as she carefully checked out the supplies in the first aid kit, and began counting the number of ban-dages they had left.

"Not that we like him any less just 'cause he can't sing," Hannah said with a smile, as cheerful a kid as always. "Because Ryan really is cool."

Feeling as though she had to defend Ryan lest the girls inadvertently or innocently share their suspicions with Ryan, Grace added, "There are plenty of song-writers out there who compose excellent music and sell their songs to people who can sing. It just takes a lot of practice to get that good, and Ryan is up here practicing and struggling to make a go of it, so we should really respect him for the effort that he is making.''

The girls nodded.

''When will you be back?'' one of the girls asked Grace as she sat down on the edge of a chair and tugged on her boots.

As soon as I find out what Ryan McCoy is really up to, Grace thought. Thankfully, due to the light snow, she had a very nice set of boot tracks to follow. ''Half an hour, probably, but don't worry if it takes me a little longer than that. In the meantime, I want you girls to finish taking your showers and then come down to the kitchen, sit at the table and either sketch or write about something we've seen on our trip so far.''

''Including the blizzard and stuff like snowflakes, or just the historical stuff we've seen so far?'' Clara asked.

Grace smiled. ''Anything you like. But Hannah's in charge. And when I get back, after lunch maybe you can all go outside and play in the snow. All right?''

''Cool.''

''Way cool.''

''Be careful, Miss Tennessen.''

''Yeah, don't get lost.''

''I won't,'' Grace promised. Not with Ryan Mc-Coy's tracks taking her right where she wanted to go.

WITH A PUSH OF A BUTTON, Ryan opened the reinforced steel door disguised as a rough-hewn rust-colored cave wall and slipped out of the room that had been surreptitiously built in the side of the mountain. Another push of a concealed electronic button closed the door behind him. Already turning up his collar against the wind, he stalked across the hidden mountainside cave to the narrow entrance. Standing just inside it, immersed in shadows, was the oh-so-familiar figure of a woman. Ryan's spirits plummeted even as his pulse soared. Damn, he thought, of all the complications he didn't need....

"If I hadn't just seen it, I wouldn't believe it," Grace exclaimed, still eyeing him with a mixture of suspicion and fury. Because now she knew for certain he had lied to her about the reason he'd left the farmhouse.

"What are you doing here?" Grace demanded.

Ryan grimaced. This was not a discussion he wanted to have with her, and certainly not at the entrance to the cave where they could possibly be overheard. "I could ask the same of you," he told her grimly as he grabbed her wrist and marched her away from the natural thicket of pine and cedar that all but obscured the entrance to the cave.

"Furthermore, what is behind that wall I just saw you walk out of?" she asked testily. She shook loose from his grasp and planted both hands on her slender hips. "What is going on here?"

"Nothing you need to know about," he told her gruffly, then sucked in his breath and fought for calm.

"I'll be the judge of that." Grace advanced toward the wall, but before Ryan could get to her, she reached behind a perpendicular ledge of rock and activated the button.

Grace gasped as the heavy door slid open. She drew in her breath sharply. "What is this?" she whispered, stunned. While Grace studied the array of videotaping and audiotaping equipment the Bureau had paid him to set up, Ryan cast a furtive glance behind them. He shut the door behind them with another push of an electronic button. He turned back to her calmly. To his relief, Grace did not seem to be at all alarmed to be confined in the room with him. Maybe because she already knew in her heart of hearts that he was there to protect and defend, not harm her.

"Where are the girls?" he asked quietly, noting the wind had mussed her golden hair and loosened long, silky strands from the prim knot on the top of her head.

"Back at the farmhouse."

Thank heaven for small miracles.

Ignoring the need to run his hands through her hair and lovingly restore some order to the wind-tossed strands of gold silk, Ryan ordered her quietly, "You need to forget what you've seen here and go and join them."

Grace tipped her head back to better see into his face. A mixture of curiosity and resentment glimmered in her jade green eyes. Pink color heightened the fair skin of her cheeks as she ever so slowly and thoughtfully raked her teeth over her lower lip.

"You're right," Grace conceded finally, as she assumed a defiant posture and folded her arms in front of her. "I need to get myself and my girls out of here now."

"Nothing would make me happier, believe me," Ryan noted with gruff honesty, "but given the condition of the roads, that's impossible."

Grace acknowledged his viewpoint with a shrug of her slender shoulders, but did not take her eyes from his as she inched off her gloves. "Via my truck, yes," she conceded with a wry smile. "But not—" she met his eyes pointedly "—if I call the sheriff and ask for immediate transport out by helicopter."

Ryan felt alarm at her boldly voiced statement. Such a move would alert Hindale and his group to the presence of seven children and an adult female, who—thanks to their run-in with Hindale on the road at the beginning of the snowstorm—the terrorist group already knew about.

You didn't need a course on domestic terrorism to figure out what Hindale's next move would be, Ryan thought grimly. He and his cronies would immediately attempt to capture and hold Grace and her girls prisoner to keep the Federal agents at bay. And while Ryan could outwit and outmaneuver them for a while, with Hindale's stockpiled weapons and superior forces and Grace and the girls' complete inexperience in defending themselves in life-and-death situations, it was inevitable someone would get badly hurt—if not killed. He didn't want to see that happen to any of the Peach Blossom Academy girls in his charge. He didn't want to see it happen to Grace.

She started to step past him, to head for the door.

He mentally girded himself and moved with her. "I'm afraid I can't let you do that."

"Why," Grace said, baiting him. "Afraid of what I'll say about you to the sheriff's office?"

"Very afraid, as a matter of fact."

"Well, too bad." Grace's voice was ice. "You should've thought of that before you lied to me about where you were going this morning and what you were going to be doing."

"Given all this," Ryan gestured vaguely behind him, "I had no choice but to lie to you."

Her delicately arched brow lifted. "We all have choices, Ryan," she said, failing to suppress a shiver that ran the length of her slender body. "You just made the wrong one."

Ignoring the urge to take her in his arms and hold her until she was warm again all over, Ryan responded to her accusation impatiently, "I'm running an investigation here, all right?"

Grace gave him a disbelieving look. "Really."

Ryan ignored the pressure building at the front of his jeans. "Yes, really," he confirmed brusquely.

Grace continued to stare at him as she rubbed her hands up and down her forearms. "All right, I'll bite," she said finally. "Who is this investigation for?"

Ryan was silent a long moment. Though he wanted to confide in her and tell her everything, he wanted to keep her safe more. And the less she knew about what he was doing, the safer she would ultimately be.

"That's not important, Grace."

She unbuttoned the front of her coat and held back

the edges with the hands she propped on her slender hips. "It is to me."

He pushed past her to the row of computers and surveillance screens that pictured the road that ran past the farmhouse he was residing in, much of the adjacent Hindale farm and the jointly owned meadow between the two properties.

"You already know a lot more than you need to," Ryan told her tersely, trying not to notice how delicately the wool trousers she wore molded to the gentle curves of her hips and thighs.

"I'll be the judge of that," she countered fiercely, following him. She edged around in front of him, so he had no choice but to stare down into her face. "Right now I think I need to know a lot more," she said airily. "So who are you working for?"

"I can't tell you," Ryan repeated.

"Then you're not a cop," Grace asserted very, very softly. "And if you're not a cop, you must be some sort of criminal." She whirled away from him and headed toward the electronic switch that controlled the door.

She had nearly reached it when Ryan caught her arm and swung her back around to face him so swiftly the momentum had her colliding with the hardness of his chest. Immediately she raised both her hands to push against his chest. "Let me go!" she said hysterically as the two of them embarked in a passionate struggle.

He gripped her arms and pulled her up against his

hard length. "As soon as you listen to me, dammit, I will."

Abruptly, Grace went very still in his arms. Ryan felt her fear, and guilt flooded him anew. *This was not what he wanted.*

"I'm not going to harm you or the girls," he told her, "but you're right to suspect danger on the mountain and plenty of it."

At his ominous words, Grace began to tremble, and desperate to comfort and cajole her in any way he could, Ryan pulled her closer still.

"What kind of danger?" Grace asked.

A picture was worth a thousand words. "Look." Ryan guided her to the high-power telescope, focused in on the Hindale farm, and when he had the picture he wanted, let her see.

Grace looked into the lens, then did a double take at the sight of ten people in combat fatigues. "Is that a tank parked in their barn?" She was incredulous.

"Yes, and it was stolen from the United States Army."

Grace gasped and laid a hand across her heart. The color left her face as she whispered faintly, "Oh, my God."

Because Grace looked as if she needed steadying, Ryan wrapped his arms around her waist. "We think they're planning to use it in an assault against the government," he told her calmly, aware he had never let a woman deter him from his work the way he was letting Grace deter him now.

Her fingers curled into the open edges of his down coat. "When? Where?" she gasped.

Ryan soothed her by running his palms up and down her back. "We don't know. That's what we're trying to find out." The last he had heard, they'd narrowed it down to three possible targets, all in the Blue Mountain Gap area of Virginia, and would choose which one was most feasible at the time.

"Does the sheriff know about this?"

"No." Ryan switched positions with her, sat down on the corner of the sturdy wooden conference table that was serving as his desk and pulled her into the V of his spread legs. Infinitely more comfortable, he continued sternly, "And we can't call him, either."

Still studying him in confusion, Grace asked, "Why not?"

Ryan laced a protective arm about her shoulders. "Because we think someone in the sheriff's department is also in the group. You and the girls will be safe, but only if you do exactly as I say and forget everything you've seen here this morning."

A contemplative silence fell between them once again. Ryan took one of her hands in his and laced his fingers tightly through hers. She looked down at their hands for a long moment, then finally lifted her face to his in silent supplication.

"You really want to protect me and the girls, don't you?" Grace whispered, her eyes full of gratitude and relief and something else that he chose not to identify.

"Yes, I do," Ryan replied hoarsely. And he would do so with his life if necessary.

Grace swallowed and shifted positions, insinuating herself even closer against his spread thighs. The heat that had been pooling in his groin spread upward in galvanizing waves. It was all Ryan could do not to groan at the feel of her sweet little bottom nestled against him.

"I'm sorry I followed you." She turned to see his face better.

Ryan grinned, realizing the danger facing them now was of an entirely different kind. "So am I," he told her gently, lifting a hand to caress her face, before he continued as grimly as before. "You would've been better off not knowing any of this, should we meet up with Hindale again."

Her chin took on a stubborn tilt, and her jade green eyes glittered with indignation. "I won't give you away!" she vowed.

"Perhaps not deliberately," Ryan agreed, knowing that as bright and quick and determined as Grace was, she was not prepared for the danger that lay ahead.

"Not at all, Ryan," Grace disagreed.

Ryan fervently hoped that was so.

Aware he'd begun to touch her a bit too lovingly, albeit unconsciously, he dropped his hand from her face, but Grace made no effort to move away from her perch on his rock-hard thigh. Once again silence fell between them. Physically they were so close Ryan thought he could feel their hearts beating as one. Yet emotionally there was still so much they did not know about each other.

"Is this why you've been up on the mountain the past year?" Grace asked eventually.

Ryan nodded. "Yes."

"And this business about you writing country and western songs—"

"Is just part of the cover," Ryan confirmed, relieved to finally be able to be honest about this. "You were right last night. I know I'm a ridiculously bad singer-songwriter, and so does everyone else around these parts, although most—" he felt the corners of his mouth crook up ruefully "—are too polite to say it."

Grace blushed guiltily, and, still holding Grace's hand loosely in his, Ryan continued matter-of-factly, "That's why they're so quick to write me off and discount me as a failure and an idiot. And the fact they don't take me seriously—at least from an intellectual standpoint, makes my surveillance job a whole lot easier."

"But they're wrong," Grace surmised softly, "because you're no idiot. Instead, you're a formidable opponent."

Ryan shrugged and let her compliment slide. He knew he was well trained and competent, but considering himself to be more than that and letting his ego get in the way of job performance could hinder him immensely. Right now, that was a risk he couldn't afford to take. "An opponent who now has a teacher and seven little girls to protect," he reminded.

Grace's soft, unglossed lips tensed as she frowned. "I'm sorry I put you in this position." She heaved an enormous sigh that raised and lowered her chest, then pushed to her feet. She turned to face him, and at the same time took a step back, so their bodies were close but no longer touching. She swallowed hard, and her eyes met his. "I'm sorry I put all of us in this position."

"You didn't mean to," Ryan soothed, knowing beating one's self up about something that was a fact had never helped anything.

"No, but it doesn't change things, does it?" Grace continued, troubled, as she began to pace about the stone-floored room. "We're in a whole lot of trouble."

Unable to bear seeing Grace suffer such fear and misery, Ryan surged to his feet and crossed to her side. He laced a comforting arm about her shoulders. "I'll get you and the girls out of here as soon as possible, so don't worry about that. In the meantime—" he tucked a finger beneath her chin and tilted her face up to his "—I want you to swear to me you won't tell anyone, not even your students or the headmistress at the academy, any of what you've seen here today."

Grace swallowed hard. "I won't, I promise," she said hoarsely.

Aware he had never wanted to kiss a woman more than he wanted to kiss Grace at that moment, Ryan stepped back. "Thank you."

"Ryan—"

The soft entreaty in her voice had him turning back around, though he intended to move away from her.

She stopped him by placing a light hand to his arm.

That close to her, wanting her so badly it was nearly

killing him, it was all he could do not to groan in outright agony. "Yes?"

"About what you said. Last night. About us not kissing again unless I initiated it."

This time he did groan, ever so softly, in regret. His whole body tense with the effort to contain his desire for her, he drew a breath and rasped, "Yes?"

"As much as I'm loath to admit it," Grace whispered as she stood on tiptoe and brushed a kiss across his cheek. "I think you were absolutely right in your prediction. I think," she murmured as her eyes darkened and she brushed the tip of her index finger across his lips, "that this is one prediction you were absolutely right about."

Abruptly, her expression sobered, and she said with a tantalizingly soft voice that teased his senses and inflamed his soul, "Before I leave here, I *will* kiss you again."

Chapter Six

"That being the case," Ryan said, taking Grace all the way into his arms, nuzzling the curve of her neck, his breath soft against her ear, "why wait?"

The next thing Grace knew, he had shifted her backward against a nearby wall, stepped neatly between her legs and fitted his tall, strong body snugly against the length of hers. His head was lowering, hers was lifting. Their eyes met. And then their lips touched in an explosion of heat unlike anything she had ever felt or dreamed. She clutched at his shoulders and kissed him back, knowing that, as desperate as he was to get them out of there, this chance might never come again. And even when his hands slipped across her ribs, to part the edges of her coat, and gently cup her breasts, she didn't move away. She had never felt as seductively feminine as she did at this very moment, she had never been compelled to melt against a man in quite this way, and she wanted to explore the full potential of this one last sweet hot kiss.

Now that Grace knew who he really was and why he was here, Ryan had intended to forgo any further physical involvement with her, but having her in his arms, having her lips part in such sweet surrender and her breasts bud against his palms quickly did away with that notion. He wanted her. How he wanted her, even before she molded her lower body to the burgeoning heat of his desire.

And if he wasn't careful, he was going to end up taking her—the "last twenty-six-year-old virgin on earth"—here, on the cold stone floor of this surveillance room. Grace deserved a lot more than that, he reminded himself irritably as he lowered his hands back to her waist. She deserved a helluva lot more. He ended the kiss with a groan deep in his throat and said, "Grace, we can't—" Even though his pagan heart and mind were clamoring to make her his, and his body felt like it was going to explode.

"I know." Grace released a shuddering sigh as she leaned her head against his shoulder.

There were so many reasons why, the least of which was the girls waiting for them back at the farmhouse. She tilted her head back to his. "But I want to make love with you," she said softly, deciding for both their sakes to end the pretending between them on every level. "And if we both didn't have such pressing responsibilities I *would* have a fling with you here and now."

She had expected her blindly adoring pronouncement to be met with joy and adulation. Instead, his face became set and grim as he silently led them out of the cave and back into the open.

"You're upset I was so—" Grace gulped "—forthright."

That was the problem growing up in an all-girls boarding school, Grace thought, struggling to keep up with him as they wound their way through the woods that separated his farmhouse from the cave.

She'd been deprived of years of normal adolescent interaction with the opposite sex, the teasing and talking and tormenting each other and just plain dealing with each other that went on as most men and women grew up.

And that, in turn, had left her at a distinct disadvantage when it came to dealing with the opposite sex. She never knew quite what to say. She either was too standoffish, like a prim and proper prude. Or she revealed too much of what she was thinking and feeling and came off looking like an idiot—in this case, a sexstarved idiot.

Ryan frowned and took her elbow as they maneuvered a particularly tricky, treacherously icy spot. "It's not that. You can speak your mind any time you want."

"Then what is it?" Grace demanded as she temporarily lost her footing and fell against him.

He cupped her elbows and let her lean against him until she steadied herself. "I may seem like a funloving good old boy with an eye for the ladies, but I still have standards, okay?" He looked down at her seriously as he let her go. "I don't have 'flings' with rookies."

"Rookie!" she repeated incredulously, putting up a

hand to shade her face from the continuing precipitation.

His face set stubbornly, Ryan led them through the woods. "And I won't take advantage of you like that, or any other beginner for that matter," he said softly but firmly.

Grace went right and Ryan went left as they both dodged a towering pine. "No wonder you're not married," she grumbled cantankerously.

Ryan suddenly took her by the shoulders and backed her up against the trunk of a nearby oak tree. He braced a hand on either side of her, effectively pinning her in place. "Look, I know the danger we're in is making you want to turn to me, in the same way that it's making me want to comfort you. But you've waited a long time for this, and your first time should be with someone you love, someone who loves *you* just as passionately. It shouldn't be something done on a whim."

Grace averted her glance as she struggled to hide her hurt. *Is that what he thought he was to her, a whim? Was that what she was to him?*

"Fine," she snapped, blinking hard to keep the tears from her eyes as her heart stopped and then resumed a jerky rhythm that left her feeling breathless and out of sorts. "We won't do anything on a whim."

But it wasn't for lack of wanting to, on her part. Which was kind of funny, she thought with more than a trace of irony. That she—a person who rarely, if ever, took the kind of personal and emotional risks they were talking about—had finally decided to just go with her feelings and her desire, only to be turned down flat, in exactly the way she had always feared she would be if she acted spontaneously.

As they trudged back in the direction of the farmhouse, Grace shoved her hands in the pockets of her wool coat.

Ryan studied her with an openness—and a frustration—that had her swallowing. "I've hurt you, haven't I?" he said at last.

"What would make you think that?" Grace forced herself to keep walking and look straight ahead. She estimated they had another half mile or so before they reached the farmhouse.

"I don't know," he said wryly, taking her by the shoulders and turning her to face him once again. "Maybe the color here—" he gently touched her cheeks "—and the tears glittering in your eyes."

Pretending a calmness of spirit she couldn't begin to feel, Grace kept her hands in her pockets and stared up at him. "It's the cold."

"Right."

Another silence fell. Ryan clamped the edges of his teeth together. "I know what we just felt seems real, Grace." Still frowning, he dropped his hands from her shoulders and stepped back.

"But you don't think it is."

"No." He folded his arms in front of him. "And you want to know why?"

"I have a feeling that even if I said no, you'd tell me."

"You're right, I would," he agreed.

"So?" she prodded, when he didn't continue right away.

He leaned closer, until she had no choice but to inhale the clean, wintry scent of his skin and hair. The guilt he felt was evident on his face.

"It happened four years ago," he said in a low voice rife with self-recrimination as they began to walk once again. "I was on another assignment, and I had a female partner. We were undercover for nearly a year."

Grace was silent, taking the information in as their footsteps crunched on the snow- and ice-encrusted ground.

"We were very attracted to each other. And as the case wore on, we got closer emotionally, as well. By the time the case ended, we were engaged to be married."

He didn't look happy about any of this, Grace noted uneasily. "Did you marry her?" she asked anxiously.

"No." Ryan frowned as he focused on the end of the woods up ahead. He stopped walking and turned to face her. "We called it off when we realized that our involvement was driven largely by the emotions aroused by the dangerous situation, and we weren't in love after all." He moved forward until they stood toe-to-toe, and took her two hands in his. His expression was both tormented and kind. "The point is, Grace, I've been there," he told her gently. "I know how much it hurts to realize that what you thought you'd felt is really only an illusion." He tightened his grip on her gloved fingers. "I don't want you to suffer the same."

Grace released a lengthy sigh. What he said made sense. Unfortunately it did not square with the feelings inside her. Feelings that were telling her to throw caution to the wind and pursue this attraction to Ryan for all it was worth, before another chance to love someone slipped through her fingers. "I suppose I should feel grateful you're going to such extremes to protect me," she said with a weariness that came straight from her soul.

"But you don't."

Her lower lip trembled. "You want to know the truth?"

"Yes."

Her frustration mounting, she tilted her head up at him, and that was when she realized it didn't matter what she wanted here, Ryan was going to do what he thought best for them regardless of anything she said or the way she felt.

Her lips tightening, she confided in a low, furious voice, "Your oh-so-noble actions remind me of my parents, when I was growing up." And the hurt over that was still with her to this very day!

Ignoring the furrowing of Ryan's brow, Grace continued, "They tried to protect me from the constant reassignment and upheaval caused by their military careers by putting me in boarding school from an early age." And as a result, the only place that was truly "home" to her, even now that she was all grown up, was a boarding school environment.

He regarded her impatiently. "Obviously it was an unhappy experience—"

"Not unhappy, necessarily." After all, she'd been clothed and fed and well educated in luxurious surroundings. "Just lonely!" Grace corrected stormily. "Though I doubt you could understand just *how* lonely, growing up the way you did. Nevertheless, there's one thing you need to know about me," she said softly, aware she was dangerously close to tears.

"I'm listening."

"I don't want to be protected by being pushed away, even if I do understand all the reasons behind such an action." She'd had enough of that, growing up. More than enough, actually.

He regarded her penitently. "Grace," he murmured as he extended a hand in abject apology.

His pity was something she did not need. Nor did she want to continue discussing her Achilles' heel. Ignoring his attempt to touch her and make peace between them, she lifted both her hands in a silencing gesture. "I've said all I have to say, Ryan."

In addition, they were clear; there would be no further emotional involvement, no more kissing, between them.

Now that Ryan was privy to her deepest vulnerability in a way no one else on earth was, she pivoted on her heel and stomped away from him. Aware he was still standing behind her, studying her contemplatively, she headed for the farmhouse without looking back.

"Is something going on between you and Ryan?" Hannah asked the moment Grace walked in the back door.

She slipped off her coat, noting that all seven girls had showered and dressed for the day in warm wool slacks and sweaters emblazoned with the school insignia. "Why would you ask that?"

The girls giggled. Letticia spoke up, "We were w-w-watching through the window."

"Yeah," Darlene spoke up, too. "And the way he was looking at you just now—"

"We thought he looked all mushy when he was standing by the woods," Polly informed her as she tugged on both her braids.

"Like he wanted to write a love song about you or something," Greta said, pushing her thick glasses higher on the bridge of her nose.

"Well, he didn't write any songs about me in the woods just now," Grace said hotly. "And I'm sure he won't in the future, either." Despite what had happened between them, despite what she had revealed about herself and her own emotions in the cave.

And that hurt a lot, even though she would've preferred not to admit it. For one brief second, when Ryan was holding her in his arms and kissing her so passionately, she'd thought—hoped—they had found something special.

Aware the girls were all watching her carefully from their places at the kitchen table, Grace turned the attention back to them. "I see you girls all got your showers," she noted approvingly. Not that she'd had any doubts that her wishes would be carried out; the girls from the Academy were a well-behaved group.

"Yep," seven-year-old Brianna took her thumb out of her mouth long enough to say. "And we're working on our remembrances of the trip."

Grace paused to look over the sketches and short stories and journal entries the girls had been creating since they had embarked on their winter break vacation. "You're all doing a super job," she said admiringly. They were a very talented group. As for their host...

Grace glanced out the window at Ryan, who was busy shoveling snow away from the house. He was simultaneously taking care of business and behaving as if he hadn't a care in the world, she noted grimly.

It was up to her to do the same.

RYAN AND GRACE managed to avoid crossing paths the rest of the morning, which was good, since Ryan had major pangs of guilt for the way he had wounded Grace to the quick.

He knew she thought he was being cruel and selfish, refusing to get involved with her, but he was really only trying to do right by her. He just hoped one day she would look back on this time in her life and see that was the case. Because if she didn't, he had a feeling that her prim and proper attitude and those walls around her heart would become even more of a fortress against emotional involvement.

And whether Grace knew it or not, she was a woman who needed to be loved. A woman who needed to be married. A woman who needed to have a family of her own and her work, too. Ryan thought she was one of the best—and most patient and attentive—teachers he had ever seen.

He just hoped she would one day find someone who could make her happy as he only wished he could.

Perhaps if they'd met some other way—

But they hadn't.

And right now he couldn't tell if what they'd felt when they kissed was born out of the situation they found themselves in, or would have been there, anyway. And until they knew, Ryan thought, as he finished shoveling the drifting snow away from the house, it was best they did keep their distance, because Grace Tennessen was one person he did not want to be worse off for having known him. That honor, Ryan figured as he put up his shovel, went to trigger-happy criminals like Hindale and his cronies.

Feeling half-frozen despite his warm clothes, Ryan slipped inside the back door. The girls were seated around the table, playing an elaborate history board game.

"We already ate our lunch, but Miss Tennessen left you a sandwich in the fridge and some soup on the stove," the girls pointed out.

Ryan grabbed both, pausing only long enough to put on a fresh pot of coffee.

"Where is Grace?" he asked casually.

"In the shower. She had to wait, 'cause we used up all the hot water this morning when we took our turns."

"With seven showers in a row, I'm not surprised."

"Do you want to p-p-play the game with us?" Letticia asked.

Ryan smiled gently at the stuttering six-year-old and patted the top of her head. "Maybe later. As soon as I eat, I've got to work a little more on my song lyrics and then go back out to the barn and work on Miss Tennessen's truck. I want to get that tire fixed up for her this afternoon."

"That'll make her happy," Clara predicted.

"Yeah, she said she really wants to get out of here as soon as possible," Darlene said.

Ouch! Ryan thought, knowing he was the sole reason for that sentiment.

"But we're in no hurry to go," Greta allowed seriously.

"Yeah," Hannah agreed cheerfully, "we kind of like it here."

The truth was Ryan liked having Grace and the girls around, too. And that was a surprise. Usually, interruptions in his ability to get a job done made him really cranky.

Ryan watched the game as he ate, then got up and fixed a thermos of coffee to take with him. "Sure you don't want to wait for Miss Tennessen to come down before you go back out in the snow?" Polly asked.

Ryan pushed the thought of Grace, fresh from the shower, naked and dripping wet, from his mind. Even worse was the thought of her wrapped only in a robe.

"Hon, I'd like to, but I really need to get my chores done."

"Well, hurry it up," Brianna urged.

"Cause we m-m-miss you," Letticia said.

Ryan grinned and stood. "I guess I've got my orders," he teased as he pulled on his boots, hat and coat.

Whistling, he left the kitchen.

He went back to the cave and did some more sleuthing via telescope and video surveillance cameras, then telephoned Juliet to report the hand-to-hand combat training he had witnessed.

From there he trudged the half-mile back, often through knee-high drifts of snow, then headed to the barn, where he worked tirelessly to get Grace and the girls ready to depart.

"YOUR TIRE is repaired and back on the truck," Ryan announced as he came in through the back door around five o'clock and found Grace and the girls in the kitchen preparing dinner. "So you'll be ready to go as soon as the snow stops and the roads are clear."

Grace looked up. She flashed him a distant smile that affected him as readily as a dagger to the heart. "Thank you," she said coolly. "I appreciate that."

But not me, Ryan thought. And wondered, even as it occurred, why the notion should bother him.

After all, wasn't this exactly what he wanted? A safe, completely nondistracting, emotionally uncomplicated relationship between them?

No sooner had he shrugged out of his coat and washed up at the sink than the phone rang. As he went into the adjacent living room to get it, the girls hushed their chatter. "Ryan McCoy here."

"Hey, Ryan, it's Sue."

The second-most persistent single woman in Blue Mountain Gap.

"There's no easy way to say it, so I'll cut straight to the chase. Mandy's been calling everyone in town today, telling them you've got company—"

"I sure do," Ryan interjected cheerfully, aware both Grace and the girls were still in earshot and hanging on his every word.

"And it's a woman by the name of Grace, who just happens to be the future Mrs. Ryan McCoy you've been telling us all about?"

"Sure is," he said easily.

"I didn't believe it," Sue confided glumly.

Ryan grinned, aware—because of Grace—that he was finally going to be let off the hook by the local romancemongers. "I know you didn't—"

"No one did," Sue continued. "But when Mandy talked to Hindale and he confirmed you'd been spotted kissing a luscious blonde—well, I guess I knew my chances of snagging you just went all to heck."

"Sorry to disappoint you, Sue," Ryan said kindly, "but that's just the way it is."

"Your heart's taken," Sue supposed as Grace joined Ryan in the living room.

More than you know, Ryan thought, as he met Grace's eyes and saw the cool appraisal in their dark jade depths. "Right. So if you wouldn't mind spreading the word for me, I'd appreciate a little peace and privacy for the next few days."

"No problem." Sue promised readily enough, "I'll tell people not to call. Though except for me and Mandy no one's gotten through. Your answering machine keeps picking up."

"I've been working on some new songs about the snow," he fibbed.

Sue chuckled. "Sure you have. Anyway, I'll talk to you later. And in the meantime, you stay warm."

"You, too."

Ryan hung up the phone, then switched the answering machine on automatic, so it would answer on the first ring. He had no qualms about doing so, as no one from the Bureau would call on the public phone line.

As he turned back to Grace, he noted she had done something a little different with her hair. Instead of being in a knot high atop her head, with feathery bangs and wisps of gold escaping to frame her face, it was pulled back in a sophisticated coil at the nape of her neck. The more severe style played up the delicate features of her face and was perfectly in sync with the cool elegance emanating from her. Not for the first time that afternoon, he wondered what he had given up in walking away from her the way he had.

"You had a number of other calls," she said.

Call it his imagination, but she looked annoyed. Ryan tilted his head in the direction of the fireplace and motioned her out of earshot of the girls, who were all still quietly busy in the kitchen.

As she closed in on him, he looked down at her and said in a voice just above a whisper. "You screened the messages?"

"Sorry," Grace shrugged and continued to look as indifferent as could be. "I had to make sure no one from the Academy was trying to get through to me." She flashed a smile that did not reach her eyes and pulled a list from her pocket. "Here's a list."

Ryan scanned the list of fifteen female names. Able to imagine just how pushy and seductive some of the messages had been, he crumpled it up and leaned down to toss it into the fire.

Grace's green eyes widened with indignation as she asked, "You're not going to call any of them back?"

Ryan shrugged and retained his arrogant stance. "No need. Thanks to your presence here, the word is getting out that I wasn't joshing with 'em when I told all those women I wasn't available for either short- or long-term romance."

Grace rolled her eyes and continued to look both jealous and angry. "They must be heartbroken," she said sarcastically.

Ryan grinned, enjoying her verbal jab as much as she had enjoyed delivering it. He sauntered closer with easy, sensual grace. "And you're angry at just the thought another woman might be interested in me," Ryan countered softly.

Normally this was the kind of misconception he would use to his advantage; in his line of work, it wasn't wise to get too close to any of those around him while he was working undercover. And yet, he didn't want to hurt Grace. He didn't want her thinking he had kissed her and romanced her only as a means to an end, because it simply wasn't true.

Aware they were mere inches apart, he braced a shoulder against the mantel and tipped his head down at her. "Generally jealousy and possessiveness are not emotions I encourage, but in this case...if it helps you to realize how high the emotions running between us are...I figure it can't be all bad."

The pulse pounded in her neck as Grace said coolly, "I'm glad I could be of use to you."

He held up a hand before she could continue scolding him. "I'm not going to let you make me feel guilty about the kiss we shared in front of Hindale," he said softly, resisting the urge to take her in his arms. "In the first place it went a long way in protecting you from Hindale, whether you realize it or not. In the second place," he continued, his hot glance skimming her from head to toe, "we had a deal. And I helped you with your truck and fixed your tire, just like I said I would—"

"And I lived up to *my end* of the deal," Grace countered lightly, as she folded her arms defiantly in front of her.

"So?..." Ryan took in the twin spots of color in her cheeks and guessed there was more.

Grace's chin thrust out stubbornly. "So, when this ends—as it most certainly will—I no longer owe you a public hug and goodbye, do I?"

Ryan sighed and tried not to think what her prim and sexy presence was doing to his senses. "I guess not," he said reluctantly in his honeyed Southern drawl.

Though he couldn't help wanting her to give him one, anyway. Not for show. Or to prove a point. Or to get him off the hook with the local ladies. But because it was going to be hard for the two of them to say goodbye. Harder, he guessed, than he could even imagine. Or she realized.

Grace gave him a glare only he could see. "Good."

Silence fell between them, more intense and awkward than before. Grace nodded toward the kitchen, her expression abruptly all business. "I've got to get back to the girls."

Ryan saw the interested glances turned their way and knew he and Grace had been off whispering to each other long enough. "I'll come with you."

"I can't believe it's still snowing," Grace murmured almost disconsolately to the girls as she resumed her place at the counter, picked up where they'd left off, as if there'd been no interruption and patiently showed them how to roll out six-inch circles of dough.

Though the snow was now falling at a much slower rate—an inch every three to four hours—it was still coming down.

Ryan had an idea what she was thinking: at this rate, they would be stuck here forever. And if it hadn't been for the Hindale situation, he couldn't exactly say he'd mind.

"Well, it is the Snowstorm of the Century," Greta

pointed out, as Grace carefully transferred one circle or "tortilla" to the cast-iron skillet on the stove.

"It's also the first time we've ever had our activities canceled since I've been at boarding school," Polly said.

"Yeah, since we're already at school," Hannah told Ryan as he went over to the sink to wash his hands, "our classes are never canceled."

"Unlike the kids in public school, who get to miss every time the roads are even the tiniest bit slick," Greta complained.

Ryan grinned. "I see your point." That had to be a major drawback of boarding school.

"What smells so good?" He looked in the direction of the stove.

"Chicken t-t-tacos," Letticia replied as she took a turn rolling out the dough for homemade flour tortillas.

"What time's dinner?" Ryan asked, watching as the older girls grated cheese, sliced up tomatoes, lettuce and black olives.

Grace did not look up from the griddle. "We were hoping to dine at six."

Ryan rubbed a hand across his stubbly jaw, aware he had some making up to do, if he and Grace were going to end this time together on good terms. And he wanted that, more than he could say. "I'll shower and be right down."

"WHAT CAN I DO to help?" Ryan asked Grace, half an hour later, when he came back downstairs to join them. He was wearing a clean pair of jeans, white thermal knit T-shirt and a dark blue corduroy shirt. His golden-brown hair was damp and smelling of shampoo and had been styled with his fingers; his jaw clean shaven and scented with cologne. The day outdoors had put a rosy glow in his cheeks. He looked damn good, and Grace was uncomfortably aware of him despite herself.

Her heart pounding at his nearness, she busied herself transferring the piping-hot food to serving dishes. "Just sit down at the head of the table," Grace said, as the girls all took their places on either side of the long table.

Trying not to think how much this felt like a family dinner to her, with Ryan taking on the role of the dad, her the mom and the girls their "children," she carried the platter of warmed tortillas to the table and sat down opposite Ryan.

They joined hands, Brianna said a brief word of thanks, and then they began passing the food around. Predictably, the girls chattered incessantly, telling Ryan about their day. "We watched the weather channel again and found out the snow's supposed to stop by morning," Hannah said.

"You know what we heard on the news?" Polly said, as she stifled yet another sneeze. "There's a bride from Philadelphia that's *missing.*"

Letticia nodded vigorously. "And a m-m-mother and her little b-b-baby who are lost, too."

"Good thing we aren't still lost," Darlene said in relief.

"I'm glad everyone knows where you are, too," Ryan concurred.

"Even if we can't leave just yet," Greta added.

Clara looked at Ryan. "'Course that just gives you more time to make goo-goo eyes at—ow!" She jumped a little, then demanded irately, "Who kicked me under the table?"

"It doesn't matter," Greta said sternly.

"There are some things you just don't say," Darlene concurred seriously.

"No matter how obvious they are," Hannah added in a stage whisper.

"Girls!" Grace reprimanded, as a self-conscious flush climbed from her neck to her cheeks. "Remember your manners."

"Sorry, Ms. Tennessen," they said.

But Ryan was not willing to let the teasing from the children go unchallenged. His eyes gleaming mischievously, he turned his attention to the youthful faces around them and said, "So, you girls think I've been making goo-goo eyes at your teacher, is that it?"

"Well—" Darlene bit her lip.

"Sort of," Greta concurred.

"But it's okay," Brianna rushed to reassure him.

"'Cause she needs someone to do that, and no one has, on account of the lieutenant," Clara blurted out.

At the mention of Seth, Grace felt her spine stiffen. "Girls, I mean it. I want you to calm down right now."

"Hang on there a minute, Grace, I'm interested in

this," Ryan said. "Tell me more about this lieutenant."

"Seth was Miss Tennessen's fiancé," Darlene said soberly.

Hannah added mournfully, "He was a Navy pilot, and he was killed before they could say their vows, when his jet went down in the ocean."

A collective sigh filtered through the girls. Then Polly added, "It was real sad, too, at least that's what we heard, because she had a bridal gown and everything."

Ryan looked at Grace. She looked back at him. "I'm sorry," he said quietly. "I didn't know."

She accepted his sympathy because it was the polite thing to do. "Thank you. It was a long time ago." *A lifetime.*

"Now—" Grace stood and smiled at the faces gathered round her as she directed the evening back in a direction she could handle "—anyone for seconds?"

GRACE MIGHT HAVE FOOLED the girls this once, but she hadn't fooled him. The minute the girls were all asleep, he sought her out.

"You don't want to talk about it, do you?" Ryan asked when he found her in the laundry room folding towels and washcloths.

"Talk about what?" Grace asked indifferently as she added another warm, fluffy towel to the stack.

"Seth," Ryan replied, unable to help but think how pretty Grace looked in the simple, black jersey dress, matching tights and suede shoes she had worn at dinner.

Grace shrugged her slender shoulders aimlessly, drawing his attention to the gold brooch she had pinned just above her left breast. "There's not much to talk about."

Ryan was not so sure that was the case. He knew the talk of Seth had upset her. Whether she admitted it or not, he felt she needed to talk about it. "For me, there is." He wouldn't be able to rest until he knew she was okay.

An annoyed frown tugged at the corners of her soft, bow-shaped lips. Grace paused in the act of smoothing the wrinkles from a soft terry washcloth, before adding it to the stack of clean linens. She shot him an aggravated glance, and electricity sizzled between them as their eyes met. "If you're asking if I'm still carrying a torch for Seth that continues even after his death—"

Ryan picked up the last towel and folded it neatly before adding it to the stack. "I am."

Grace folded her arms and leaned back against the decade-old clothes dryer the Bureau had provided for Ryan via a used-furniture store. "The answer is no, although I did love him desperately."

Ryan looked at Grace, all the compassion he felt for her reflected in his eyes. "How long were you two together?"

"A little over a year. I met him during my third year of teaching at the boarding school." Looking abruptly restless, Grace glided past him and into the kitchen, where she went straight for the coffeemaker on the counter. "Initially I didn't want to get involved with Seth because he was a Navy fighter pilot and intended to stay one, and I knew any woman who got involved with him would be destined to spend great chunks of her life alone, while he was off on a mission."

Ryan watched as Grace added a paper filter and coffee grounds to the filter. "But he wore you down," Ryan guessed as he filled the reservoir with ice-cold water from the tap and then snapped it back into place.

"And I fell in love with him—" Grace continued as she switched the coffeemaker on and looked outside at the softly falling snow "—and we became engaged."

"That must have been a happy time for you," Ryan said softly, aware once again of the overpowering need to comfort her.

Grace's lips curved in a reflective smile. "You're right. It was." She turned away from the window and stood, one shoulder resting against the pane. "I wanted to get married right away, because Seth was being sent to the Middle East again for a tour. But Seth said I deserved only the best, and that meant we had to wait six months so we could have a formal wedding and perfect honeymoon and begin our married life together, under one roof, instead of thousands of miles apart."

"His protecting you that way makes sense," Ryan said as he gave in to a whim and took her hand in his.

"I thought so, too, at the time." Grace sighed and looked down at their linked fingers. "After he died, I regretted the fact that we were never together in the way we would've been as man and wife. I wished we had just said to heck with having an elaborate wedding, and gone with our feelings and eloped and made love and been together, before it was too late." Her lower lip trembled, and she shook her head as she met his gaze head-on. "I wished I'd had the chance to make love with someone I loved with all my heart and soul. But I didn't. And now of course—" she gestured helplessly, silently confirming Ryan's guess that she never talked about this with anyone "—it's too late to do anything about it."

Hence, Ryan thought sagely, *she remained, in her own dryly uttered words, "the oldest living virgin."*

"Since then," Grace confided, her spirits rising as she returned the conversation to the present day, "I've turned all my attention to the girls at the boarding school."

Ryan grinned. "To excellent result," he told her. "They all adore you."

Grace beamed beneath his praise. She wrinkled her nose at Ryan in a teasing manner. "And you, too, let's not forget."

Ryan noticed the coffee had finished brewing. He moved to get two stoneware mugs from the cupboard. "They're great kids," he noted, as he poured coffee for them both and handed her one.

"And very sympathetic to my plight," Grace said, as she got out the cream and sugar. She stirred a generous amount of both into her coffee, and they carried their cups to the kitchen table. "The bottom line is they want me married off."

Ryan sat down adjacent to her, situating himself so close to her their knees were almost touching. He picked up a walnut chocolate chip cookie from the plate in the center of the table and dipped it into his coffee. "So I'm not the first guy they've tried to pair you with."

"Nope." After some deliberation, Grace took a cookie, too. "It'd be nice if you were the last, though."

Ryan polished off the first cookie and reached for another. "Like me that much, hmm?" he quipped.

Grace flushed and ducked her head. "You know what I mean."

Ryan watched her munch on a cookie. He knew she wanted the subject closed, but he couldn't let her consider the subject closed and then spend the rest of the evening brooding over events way out of her control that had happened long ago.

More than ready to give the pep talk that was needed here, he reached across the table and covered her hand with his. It wasn't like him to get involved with other people's personal problems. Most of the time he had all he could do handling the complicated set of circumstances that went with every undercover assignment for the Bureau. But there was something about Grace he couldn't turn away from. Something about Grace that kept haunting him day and night.

He touched the side of her face. Her skin felt like hot silk beneath his fingertips. She trembled at his touch and he let his hand slide to the back of her neck. He tilted her face up to his and felt his heart pound. The way she looked at him, all soft and yearning, threw his senses into an uproar, and he knew he had to keep trying to reach her, to make her see she couldn't go through the rest of her life alone, any more than he could. "Don't be so quick to give up on romance," he said softly.

Briefly, hurt glimmered in her eyes. She pushed away from the table and surged to her feet. Coffee cup in hand, she marched to the sink and threw the dregs down the sink. "I'm just trying to be practical."

Ryan leaned back in his chair and continued to regard her steadily. "There's a man out there for you—" *And I know just who it is, he thought with a great deal of satisfaction—me.*

But, judging by the annoyed glimmer in her jade green eyes, Grace did not want to hear about his plans to court her as soon as they were both out of here and his current assignment was over.

"And, let me guess," she paraphrased for him dryly, "it's time I forgot the heartache of the past and started living in the present?"

Obviously she had heard this sentiment before. Probably from everyone who cared about her. It didn't, however, mean the advice was not worth repeating. Ryan left his coffee cup on the table, stood and sauntered across the room to her side. The urge to console her stronger than ever, he rested both hands on her shoulders. "There's plenty in life left to enjoy, Grace."

She fixed him with a cool stare. "That's not what you said to me this afternoon."

This afternoon, Ryan thought, on a surge of regret, he'd been a fool. "You can't fault me for wanting to protect you."

Grace tossed her head. "I can fault you for anything I like," she retorted emotionally.

True, Ryan thought.

And since that was the case...

"What are you thinking?" she demanded suspiciously at once.

Ryan grinned. "That since I'm already in trouble..." Ryan drew her against him and lowered his lips to hers. One touch of those smooth, sensual lips against his and he was on fire. The way she opened her mouth to his turned him to molten lava. The scent of her, so wintry and floral and clean, drove him wild. And once he felt the surrender of her body against his, once he felt the desire in the way she kissed, there was no stopping with just one kiss. No pretending that something extraordinary wasn't happening between them, because it was. They were meant to be together, he and Grace. Meant to find each other in this time and in this place.

But at the same time he knew Seth had been right about one thing. Grace deserved the best. She deserved to be married when she finally gave herself to a man.

She'd waited this long for the perfect wedding and honeymoon, and he wasn't planning to deprive her of either, no matter how much he wanted her.

Slowly he lifted his mouth from hers. Slowly he released her.

"I just want to know one thing," she said in a low, shaken voice, reproaching him softly as they stepped apart.

Forewarned by the underlying note of steel in her voice, Ryan tensed. "And what's that?" he asked, frankly curious as to how her mind worked.

"Who kissed me just now?" Grace demanded in mild exasperation, propping both hands on her hips. "Ryan McCoy, undercover agent—or Ryan McCoy, the man?"

Chapter Seven

Ryan frowned at Grace in consternation. "I don't know what you're talking about."

Grace shot him an arch look as the self-conscious flush in her cheeks deepened. "If I'm going to be kissing you," she told him sweetly, moving away from him, "I want to know where the undercover character ends and the real man begins."

Ryan lounged against the kitchen counter and studied her damp, swollen lips. Grace obviously thought there had been artifice on his part in the kisses they'd just shared, but she was wrong. Dead wrong. He knew, however, to try and convince her of this with words alone was as futile as trying to halt the snow outside, so he spread his arms wide. "What you see is what you get."

"If that were actually the case," Grace retorted coolly, refusing to be distracted by clever repartee, "then you'd be a successful songwriter—or at the very least a determined wanna-be."

Ryan frowned. This was an area he did not want to delve into, and she knew it. "We've covered that ground, Grace.'' Furthermore, he thought irritably, she knew damn well why he'd done all he had in that regard. Success in undercover work depended on the details.

''I know we have, Ryan. I'm talking about the rest of your behavior.'' Grace sauntered forward and looked him over from head to toe. ''For instance, are you really as straightforward and easygoing as you seem?''

''It depends,'' Ryan said with a cautious shrug, fairly certain from the hot gleam of temper in her eyes there was a trap somewhere in what she'd just said. ''Most of the time I am.''

''Long enough to disarm people and get what you want from them, you mean,'' Grace corrected.

Ryan ran a hand through his hair as he fought back the first stirrings of panic. Whether he liked it or not, Grace was looking for a reason to end this. He didn't want to give one to her. ''Look,'' he told her flat-out. ''I was reared in the South. Being relentlessly cheerful and accommodating, no matter what the circumstances, was the way I was brought up.''

That Grace seemed to understand. He suspected being a military brat came with its own unspoken set of expectations. A certain stoicism. A willingness to honor obligations to the best of any family's ability and accept whatever assignments came their way.

''How many undercover roles have you had?'' she asked warily.

Figuring by now that this was going to be a long inquisition, Ryan tossed out the dregs of his coffee and poured himself another cup. Finished, he turned back to her to answer her question. "Fifteen, if you include this one."

"And how many of those assignments were long-term?" Grace pressed as she began to pace restlessly back and forth.

"Seven of them lasted a year or more," he replied, trying not to be distracted by the sway of her hips beneath the clinging knit jersey fabric of her dress. He moved over to stand beside her and glance out at the winter wonderland outside. With the snow piling up to new heights, it was easy to believe they could be stranded here together for several more days, and even easier to imagine them kissing again. "The others ran anywhere from three to six months."

Grace tapped the toe of her black suede shoe flat against the floor in a thoughtful rhythm. "And for each one you had a completely different identity?"

Ryan sipped his coffee, not sure what she was getting at. He just knew she was a tiny bit afraid of him—and their fast-growing feelings for each other—and that was the last thing he wanted. "Yes."

Grace bit her lower lip, the silence resounding between them like a drum. "Did you have to lie about your family, too?"

"I usually just say I'm an orphan," Ryan replied honestly, aware all over again how much he hated deceiving ordinary people. The criminals he pursued, of course, were another matter entirely. "Doing so saves me from inventing elaborate lies that might trip me up in an unguarded moment."

"But you told the girls and me the truth?"

He studied the confusion in her eyes, hating the fact he had hurt or disillusioned her in any way. "Yes."

"Why?" Grace blurted out as they stood there, staring at each other, breathing in odd jumpy rhythms.

"I don't know." He shrugged his shoulders laconically, not used to having to explain himself to anyone in quite this way. Maybe it was because he'd felt something happening between them, even back then. Something he wanted to further.

"I see," Grace said coolly as the air between them seemed to grow thicker once again. Her pretty chin turned a notch more stubborn even as her eyes narrowed. "And what do the people here in Blue Mountain Gap, Virginia, think?"

Hell if I know, Ryan thought. He hadn't gotten close enough to any of them to find out.

"What did you tell them about your family?"

Ryan wished Grace would stop grilling him this way—as though he was an accomplished fraud she needed to expose, layer by deceptive layer, in order to protect her heart from being broken. Hadn't she figured out by now that, highly skilled at undercover work or not, he wanted only to protect her...and the girls? He stared at her in a deliberately disquieting manner and continued patiently, "I told them the usual, that I was orphaned at an early age. You and the girls are the only ones who know the truth about my family." And that was the way it would stay.

That intimate revelation, however, did little to reassure her. As flighty as a butterfly in spring, she surged away from him yet again. "And what's the truth about your name?" she murmured as she turned to face him yet again and her glance skimmed his face and lingered far too long for comfort on his lips. She wet her lips and glowered up at him. "Just a few minutes ago who was I really kissing? A Ryan, a Matt, a Jake?"

Ryan felt his body respond to her heated questioning, as easily as it had to her kiss. Aware he could hardly do what he wanted—tug her into his arms and kiss her breathless again—he drained his coffee in a single draught and set the cup aside with a frustrated thud. "What do names matter?"

Grace scowled at him suspiciously. "They just do!"

"Fine," he said, irked to be discussing such mundane matters when their feelings were at stake. He let his glance coast over the fine-boned beauty of her face, then cocked his head and considered. "Then let's just say that the man you kissed tonight was the 'real McCoy' and leave it at that, shall we?"

Grace frowned. She folded her arms in front of her, the contentious movement drawing his attention to the full, soft curves of her breasts. "This isn't a joke, Ryan," she scolded him, as the atmosphere around them became increasingly charged and electric.

"Believe me, I can see that," he said gruffly, wishing he could do what he wished and take her to bed and make passionate, endless love to her until she had no choice but to believe his feelings for her were very, very real. Instead, they were locked in a situation laced with potential danger. And Grace, unlike him, was not skilled in hiding her feelings from public view.

"So what is your real name?" Grace prodded.

Ryan had never yet drawn an unwitting civilian into one of his cases. Unfortunately he realized she was not about to give up until he told her *something* of substance. "My real first name is Ryan."

She was silent a moment, taking that in. "And Mc-Coy?" she asked warily.

"Is an alias," Ryan replied gruffly. "And for the moment," until this assignment is over, "that's all I can tell you."

As Grace's gaze meshed with Ryan's, she knew she had to ask: was she nuts, getting romantically involved with a man when she didn't even know his real last name?

Grace had to admit that normally she would have thought that to be the case. But no matter what the circumstances that had thrown them together, she couldn't believe that she was merely a convenient outlet for Ryan's long-pent-up passions, or that he was seducing her merely as a way to pass the time. He wanted to be closer to her, just as she genuinely wanted to be closer to him. It might not be wise. It might even hurt her long-term, but right now she couldn't turn away.

She took a deep breath. As trust took over, her voice gentled. "So what's the difference between the real you and the somewhat um…deluded and, let's face it, untalented songwriter you're pretending to be?"

As she'd meant him to, Ryan grinned at the note of

humor in her voice. "I suppose I'm more ambitious," he said, allowing his posture to relax, too.

"What else?" Grace asked, tipping her head back to better see his face.

Ryan took her hand and tugged her close. "I'm also more focused on my work than McCoy."

Her hard-won independence faded as he wrapped a hand around her waist. "How are you different in here?" She splayed both hands across the warm solidness of his chest and pointed to his heart.

"I don't know. I'm not sure I am any different in here." Ryan paused. "Why does this matter to you?"

Grace shrugged, reluctant to admit how afraid she was of being seduced into loving someone who would ultimately be just as inaccessible to her—emotionally and otherwise—as everyone else of importance in her life. "Because I want to know what you're really like, deep inside." *I want to know if those flashes of loneliness I see sometimes in your eyes are real or a part of my imagination, because deep down I'm lonely, too.*

Grace drew a bolstering breath. "And I want to be able to separate the real you from this role you're playing. I assume there is a clear-cut delineation dividing the two?"

Ryan frowned. "I know what you want me to say."

"But?" Grace's heart pounded as she waited for his reply.

He shook his head impatiently. "It's not that easy, Grace. I've been undercover for almost a year here. That means every day I have to eat and sleep and breathe the quest for country music stardom."

It meant, Grace thought, every day he became a little less like himself and more like the man he had created. To the point he had lost himself? "Do you even like country music?" she asked.

"Sure." He shrugged his broad shoulders indifferently. "But I like Beethoven and Mozart, too."

"But you can't listen to it here," Grace guessed.

"No—" his smile grew warm with intimacy, and his voice was almost a caress "—because it would blow my cover."

Grace ignored the caressing hand on her waist. "Is this the way you'd really dress, given your druthers?"

He shrugged and his voice was lazy and oddly content, "I'd probably wear more khaki and less flannel, but again, it would depend on what I was doing. When I'm back at Bureau headquarters, I have to wear a suit and tie."

Aware a peculiar warmth was spreading through her, due to the waves of heat rolling off his body, so comfortably aligned with hers, she tilted her head back to look up at him. She let her gaze rove the ruggedly handsome contours of his face and the clean, soft, rumpled layers of his golden-brown hair. "And your hair, if you weren't undercover, how would it be cut?"

The corners of his mouth crooked up ruefully. "Regulations dictate it be a little shorter than it is now."

That wasn't what she'd asked. She tapped him gently in rebuke. "How would you wear it if you had a choice?"

"That is my choice, to do what is necessary to hold a job with the Bureau."

"Your work means that much to you?" she said, fearing she already knowing the answer.

He nodded seriously. "For the past thirteen years, it's meant everything."

"When this is over, then what?" Grace asked, reluctantly reminding herself of a promise she'd made not to get involved with anyone whose line of work could potentially come between them. She'd already lost both a fiancé and the attention of her parents when she was growing up to the dangers and demands of military life. Common sense told her not to set herself up for more of the same.

Ryan shrugged uncaringly. "I'll be debriefed, file a bunch of reports, probably accept an award of some sort—assuming I'm successful, and head home to spend time with my family before going on to the next assignment."

Grace did her best to rein in her feelings, but Ryan's dedication to his work prompted a whole slew of memories, none of them pleasant, and the disappointed words were out before she could stop them. "So this is it for you, isn't it?" she assumed sadly, unable to suppress her sorrow that Ryan would probably never have the wife and children he deserved as long as he did this kind of work. "This is the way you're going to spend your life? Going from one dangerous situation to the other, living undercover for months at a time, pretending to be something and someone you're not?"

His golden-brown eyes went dark with anger. Apparently she wasn't the first person who'd said as much to him. "My efforts here will save lives, Grace."

"I'm not disputing that," Grace acknowledged with a heavy sigh as the two of them moved apart and regarded each other warily. "I'm just asking what cost all this will ultimately have for you."

GRACE'S WORDS haunted Ryan long after she had retired for the night. And much as he didn't want to admit it, Ryan knew Grace was right. If he kept working undercover, he would never have the wife and kids he'd always wanted. More troubling still was the notion he'd never have the kind of one-on-one closeness with a woman he'd always dreamed about.

But even if he quit the Bureau and went back to electrical engineering, getting those things was not going to be easy. The chief stumbling block was his problem with intimacy. While working undercover, he'd spent so much time trying to keep those around him at arm's length he wasn't sure he knew how to be close to anyone anymore—*if* he ever had. As he recalled, he hadn't been too good at sharing his feelings when he was a kid, either.

Grace, on the other hand, seemed to have no problem verbally expressing what was on her mind. And what she wanted was a man who would be there for her, through thick and thin—sharing, caring and taking care of her. A man whose work took second place to her in his life. Was that him? Or was this just a fantasy, engendered by the blizzard-induced confinement? As long as they were living here together, it was easy enough to imagine them a couple, with children of their own. But what would happen when the snowstorm ended and they all went back to their normal lives? Given the demands of their jobs, would he and Grace ever even see each other again? And if she weighed the odds for and against a successful relationship with someone like him and then chose not to spend any more time with him, period, how would he feel?

Ryan's doubts haunted him as he went to sleep. And they still tormented him the next morning, when he awakened to the sound of soft, scampering footsteps tiptoeing down the stairs and into the kitchen.

Ryan groaned. The good news was he didn't have to get dressed, since he'd slept in his clothes. The bad news was, he didn't want to get up. But, given the feminine voices giggling in the kitchen and the absence of Grace's low, melodious voice, it appeared he had no choice. Yawning, he stood, stretched and ambled into the kitchen to see what was going on. All seven girls were standing around in their bathrobes, pajamas and slippers. They grinned at him and giggled some more as he raked a hand through the tousled layers of his hair. "What's up?"

"We're hungry," Darlene announced.

Hannah rubbed her eyes. "And Miss Tennessen is still asleep."

"Do you think we should wake her?" Polly asked Ryan.

That decision was easy, Ryan thought. He shook his head. "No. Let her sleep. We can handle this." *I think.* He hooked his thumbs through the belt loops of his jeans. "Does anyone here know how to cook?"

The girls giggled and rolled their eyes. "We-e-e-l..."

"They don't really l-l-let us in the kitchen at b-b-boarding school," Letticia said.

"Everything is done for us," Hannah added cheerfully.

"On account of they want us to study," Clara chimed in.

"Except sometimes Miss Tennesson gives us cooking lessons," Brianna said.

"Yeah, one time she taught us how to make cookies," Darlene added. "Another, pizza, but never breakfast."

Greta peered at him curiously from behind her thick glasses. "Do you know how to cook, Ryan?"

He'd been afraid they would ask that. "I have a few specialties."

Polly sneezed three times and reached for a tissue. "Yeah, like what?" she asked.

Ryan grinned and ran a hand along his unshaven jaw. "Beefsteak and chili."

"Ugh!" the girls said in unison.

"We can't eat that for breakfast," Greta said grumpily.

"We could if we were cowboys," Hannah allowed.

Darlene went to the pantry. She plucked a brightly colored box off the shelves and waved it at him. "How about pancakes, Ryan? Do you know how to make those? 'Cause you've got a mix here you could use.''

Brianna took her thumb out of her mouth. ''And some maple syrup, too,'' she added helpfully as she plucked a bottle off the shelves.

''Well...'' Ryan took the box and studied the back of it. Truth to tell, it didn't look all that hard. He'd have preferred to feed them all cold cereal, but he wasn't sure they had enough to go around as they were getting low on milk.

Clara stared at him, puzzled, while everyone else waited for him to make a decision. ''How come you have all these different kinds of foods if you don't know how to cook 'em?'' she asked finally.

Because the Bureau sent out the groceries along with the rest of my ''stuff'' via moving van, Ryan thought. *And they wanted it to look as though I did know how to cook and was settling in to stay awhile.* But he couldn't very well tell them that. Aware the girls were still waiting for answers to their questions, Ryan finally said, ''I was planning to learn how to cook when I got around to it. And no, I've never made pancakes, but I reckon we could do it if we all put our minds to it.''

''Maybe we could even surprise Miss Tennessen with breakfast in bed,'' one of the girls said.

The thought of Grace snuggled in the covers caused a heat in Ryan equaled only by the curiosity about what kind of nightclothes she was currently wearing.

Deciding in this case that restraint was the better part of valor, he winked at the girls. ''Nice thought, girls, but I think, in this case, we'll just wait for Sleeping Beauty to join us.''

SUNLIGHT STREAMED into the room, bathing Grace in a bright white light as she squinted and looked toward the window. The first thing she noticed, when her eyes finally adjusted to the glare, was the fact it had stopped snowing and the clouds had disappeared. The second, that it was nine o'clock!

She blinked, sure she'd read the clock wrong, then groaned, realizing she had overslept by several hours. This was definitely not good when she had seven girls on a field trip to command. Jump-started by the worry over what mischief they could be into, she leaped from the bed and rushed into the bathroom. Completing her morning ablutions in record time, she grabbed her bathrobe and headed for the two rooms where the girls were bunked down.

Both bedrooms were empty, just as she had feared. Still pulling a brush through the tangled length of her golden hair, Grace headed swiftly downstairs. She hoped the girls hadn't awakened Ryan. She didn't really want to face him after the way their conversation had ended last night. But it was much too late for that, she realized regretfully as she saw the empty sofa, heard the series of giggles and smelled the delicious aroma of pancakes and warmed maple syrup coming from the farmhouse kitchen.

Ryan was awake and standing at the stove, looking deliciously rumpled and unshaven and flipping pancakes like an experienced chef. As for the rest of the kitchen, Grace thought, as she dropped her hairbrush into the pocket of her robe, it was an unqualified disaster. In fact, Grace was sure she had never in her life seen such a mess. Pancake mix, eggs, milk and oil were spilled over the countertops. Innumerable mixing bowls and spoons had been dirtied.

"Hey, look, it's Sleeping Beauty!" Clara giggled.

Grace flushed and touched a hand to her hair as she realized they were talking about her. "That's what Ryan was calling you," Clara explained.

Ryan looked at Grace. Grace looked at Ryan. Sparks flew between them as their eyes met. "You know me," he said offhandedly, seemingly unable to tear his eyes from her face. "Anything for a laugh."

Grace nodded, feeling unutterably embarrassed, as her hand went to the belt on her robe. Her throat feeling as dry as the Sahara—yet again—she turned back to the girls. She forced herself to concentrate, as any good instructor from The Peach Blossom Academy would, on the basics of decorum. "Did you thank Ryan for cooking you breakfast?" she asked with a polite smile that felt as forced and pleasant as did her voice.

"Thank you, Ryan!" they all chirped obediently.

Darlene checked the time on the clock, looked outside, then back at Ryan. "Now that Miss Tennessen is up can we go and get dressed?" she inquired, unable to contain her excitement.

"Yeah, now that it's stopped snowing we want to start shoveling the driveway right away!" Hannah added cheerfully.

Polly bounced from foot to foot, like a runner about to start a race, as she turned her enthused glance to Grace and explained, "We made a deal with Ryan. He said he'd cook us all breakfast if we'd help clear a path from the barn to the road."

Grace turned back to Ryan. He lifted his broad shoulders in a lazy shrug. "I figured we better work on that, so you can get out of here as soon as they get the snowplows out this way and get the roads clear," he explained.

Grace's heart turned over at the thought of leaving, but for the girls' sake she worked hard to keep her expression serene. "How long do you think that will be?" she asked.

"Hard to say." Ryan shrugged again and cleared his throat. "Given the enormous amount of snow, I doubt they'll get the road cleared today, but maybe by tomorrow or the next day they will," he said softly, adding as an afterthought, "if we're lucky."

Lucky wasn't how Grace would describe it. Though she could hardly blame Ryan for wanting to get rid of all of them. They had disrupted his life, interfered with his work.

Brianna teared up. "I don't want to leave you, Ryan," the normally bashful seven-year-old announced, as she moved forward and grabbed on to his leg.

My feelings exactly, Grace thought, as Ryan reached down and gently tousled Brianna's hair. He was probably thinking, Grace recalled, that at first Brianna had been terrified to stay. But she'd warmed up to Ryan, to the point she was participating more in group conversations and activities, and sucking her thumb a little less.

"Yeah. Can't we spend the rest of our winter vacation here?" Greta asked. "After all, it's still snowing really bad practically everywhere, even in Kentucky. They said on the news they'd never had that much snow there!"

Grace interrupted. "Now girls, we've imposed on Mr. McCoy long enough. Besides, we have a lot left to see and do, including our tour of Colonial Williamsburg. And eventually the roads from here to there will be clear."

Around her, faces fell. Aware they weren't the only ones who did not want to leave Ryan, Grace pushed her own melancholy away. She had to set an example here.

"Is it okay if we get ready to go outside?" Darlene asked impatiently.

Grace tacitly nodded her permission. She might be a novice at romance and dealing with the opposite sex, but being a schoolteacher was something she knew how to do.

"Everyone wear your thermal underwear and bundle up. You older girls help the younger ones, okay? And I want those rooms straightened before you go out."

Their orders received, the girls raced off in a giggling, chattering group. Ryan wordlessly poured her a cup of coffee and handed her that, a spoon and a jar of nondairy creamer. "You look like you need this almost more than I do," he teased.

"Thanks," Grace said, rolling her eyes and trying not to notice the tingle that went through her every time they touched.

He looked into her eyes, the expression in his moving from joshing to unbearably tender and solicitous in an instant. "Sleep well?" he asked softly.

Grace stirred in two spoonfuls of powdered white creamer with a hand that felt trembly and hot, and then set the spoon in the sink. "Not particularly," she said as she looked down into her cup. She had tossed and turned all night, then finally fallen into a deep sleep around 6:00 a.m.

He sipped his coffee, too. "Neither did I."

She swallowed hard around the knot in her throat as the two of them lounged against the counter, side by side. "I'm sorry I overslept," she said, watching as he carefully poured another batch of silver-dollar pancakes on the griddle.

Finished, he set the mixing bowl aside and turned back to her with a look of masculine appreciation and a ready smile. "No problem," he said as his gaze roamed over her from head to foot, then returned at leisure to linger on her upturned face.

You'd think from the way he's looking at me, that I'm the most beautiful woman on earth.

Grace struggled to ignore the sexual heat in his golden-brown eyes—it was causing her breasts to tighten, turning her knees to gelatin and making an unassuaged ache well up in her middle. She took another sip of coffee. "Why are you looking at me like that?"

He reached out to stroke a hand through the hair that lay across her shoulders. "I've just never seen you with your hair down," he confided huskily, as even more warmth crept into his eyes and a sexy smile drifted across his face. "You look...different."

Grace flushed self-consciously, realizing he was right, she usually did wear her hair up. If she hadn't been in such a hurry to get downstairs and check on the girls, she would have pinned it up this morning. "Oh."

"I like it down, though," he continued, wrapping his fingers in the ends, rubbing them softly. "It's softer. Sexier. Younger."

She felt softer, sexier, younger. And Grace hadn't felt this way since she couldn't remember when. "When you look at me that way, you make me feel about sixteen," she told him.

He paused to flip the pancakes. "Is that a bad thing?"

I'm not sure. Grace watched him put the spatula down. "In what sense?" she feigned cool implacability, aware her heart was beating very fast, and her thoughts were definitely not tame.

"Does it feel like a bad thing?" he persisted, running a hand down the side of her face.

With effort Grace drew a trembling breath and moved away from his devastatingly tender touch. "Let's put it this way," she said, drawing another ragged breath at the banked fires she saw in his eyes. "If I'm sixteen, you ought to be rated NC-17."

He laughed, soft and low, and looked to her at that moment as free of spirit and wild at heart as she felt. With a sigh, Ryan winked and reluctantly moved away. "I guess I better feed you before we get ourselves in trouble."

Grace told herself it was not disappointment she was feeling as he took the last batch of golden-brown pancakes off the griddle. After all, she hadn't expected him to kiss her again this morning—had she?

"Care for some pancakes?" he asked.

Grace nodded. "Thanks." Still struggling to regain her equilibrium, Grace plucked some silverware from the drawer, carried her plate to the table and sat down.

Ryan brought a pitcher of juice from the refrigerator, and a glass to the table for her. "I'd offer you milk," he announced lazily, "but we're out."

Grace's brow furrowed as the impact of his words sank in. "Wait a minute. We had a whole gallon left last night."

"Right. And the girls drank it all for breakfast."

Grace bit her lip at this new reminder of how they had disrupted his life. "Oh, dear. I didn't mean for that to happen. I was planning to ration it."

"It's okay." Ryan waved off her concern as he opened the freezer compartment and pointed to the dozen juice cans stacked inside. "We've got tons of water and plenty of frozen concentrate left."

But the fact remained, Grace thought, as Ryan brought a plate to the table for himself, they were beginning to run out of select items of food. She could only hope that was the biggest problem they would encounter before she left.

He sat down opposite her. Grace was oddly pleased he had waited to eat his meal with her. "Thanks for making breakfast for everyone," she said.

Ryan spread a lavish amount of butter and syrup on his pancakes before he dug in. "I enjoyed it," he told her, after they'd both had a bite or two of the delicious pancakes. "Though I gotta say," he continued, after a gulp of juice, "there was a moment or two there when I thought my foray into the culinary arts might turn into an unqualified disaster. Making up the batter was no problem once we found the ingredients in the cupboards—the directions on the box of pancake mix were pretty specific. But cooking the hotcakes was another matter entirely."

Recalling, he shook his head and rolled his eyes in aggravation. "The first batch cooked all the way through but they were sort of pale and wimpy looking, so I turned up the heat till water danced on the griddle and ended up burning the second batch. So then I turned down the heat a tad, and the next batch turned out golden brown."

"That's par for the course," Grace told him with a grin. "The first batch is never as good as the ones that follow—something about preparing the griddle, I think."

He studied her over the rim of his coffee cup. "You like to cook?"

"Mmm-hmm. It's one of my hobbies," Grace admitted with a smile. "I give cooking lessons to the girls at school."

"Yeah," Ryan said with a grin as he got up to retrieve the coffeepot. "The girls said something about that."

Grace caught the teasing glimmer in his eyes and knew there was more. "What else did they say?" she prodded, sure it was of an embarrassing nature.

"Oh," Ryan said magnanimously as he leaned back in his chair, "there were lots of hints about Valentine's Day—that it's just a month away, and you don't currently have a boyfriend but you'd probably like one. And let's see, what else? Oh, yeah, they think we'd make a really cute couple," he reported smugly.

Grace groaned as telltale heat swept into her cheeks. Throughout the rest of her, a different kind of tension built. "I can't believe this," she complained, embarrassed beyond belief. "That's all you need. Us here—" *When you're trying to do a job.* "Plus matchmaking."

He flashed her a totally devastating and guileless smile. "It'd be even better if I thought that matchmaking was going somewhere."

Grace swallowed around the sudden tightness in her throat. And the answering beat of her heart. "Ryan—"

"It's stopped snowing and—according to the latest weather report this morning—the cold front that brought the blizzard is nearly past us. Soon our enforced confinement on the farm will be over, too. But *we* don't necessarily have to be, Grace." Without warning he leaned forward and captured her hands in his.

Grace blinked. "You're saying you want to see me after this is all over?" she asked, feeling both wary and stunned.

Ryan nodded. "That's exactly what I'm saying."

Chapter Eight

"I don't know what to say," Grace whispered softly as her heart began to pound and her hopes continued to soar.

His eyes turned a dark, liquid gold. "Say yes," he whispered tenderly, as he stood, took her hand and drew her to her feet.

Grace floated into his embrace.

"Say yes," he whispered again as he framed her face with his hands and tilted her head up to his.

Her breath stalled in her throat, even as her eyelids fluttered down. "Oh, Ryan—" Grace's breath whispered out in a wistful sigh, and then all rational thought was lost as his morning beard ever so gently abraded her face and his lips touched hers. He tasted of sweet maple syrup and coffee, and the warmer dusky flavor that was him. He exuded love and tenderness and the gentle sexiness that was so much a part of his charm. And he felt so warm and strong and solid. Like a man she could lean on, like a man who would be there for her through thick and thin.

Forgetting for a moment all the reasons why they

shouldn't get more involved, Grace stood on tiptoe, wreathed her arms around his neck and kissed him back, warming and melting like snow beneath the winter sun. He was too good at this, too good at taking a moment that should have been awkward and difficult and making it seem natural and right. He was too expert with his kisses, too skilled in rousing her passion and her emotions.

She wanted him. Oh, how she wanted him, and it was at that moment, as she leaned into him all the way and fervently returned his kiss that she realized—as abruptly as he—that they were no longer alone. Behind them, the girls were giggling and whispering.

Flushing, Grace and Ryan moved apart.

Grace was stunned to realize she'd been so caught up in Ryan's sweet, tender kiss she hadn't even heard her students come downstairs. But they didn't seem to mind.

"Uh—sorry to interrupt, but we're ready to go outside and start shoveling snow now. So, is it okay?" Hannah asked.

Grace knew she should say something about what they'd just witnessed, but at the moment nothing appropriate came to mind. "It's fine," she said in a strangled voice as she turned away and tried to hide her embarrassment.

The girls tromped on outside, their voices carrying behind them. "See, I told you they were having a romance," Polly said.

"You mean starting one," Greta added.

Darlene sighed dreamily. "It's like they were always meant to be together."

"Did you see the way they look at each other?" Clara asked the group softly, astounded.

"Yeah, and it's all so romantic," Darlene agreed.

The girls's voices faded.

"I guess that means they like you," Grace said pleasantly. She tried not to think what their approval meant to her as she carried their dishes to the sink and set them down next to it.

Ryan grabbed her by the robe and tugged her close. "I guess they do," he said gruffly, looking down at her once again. "But as fond as I'm beginning to be of all of them—" he said as his thumbs stroked first her cheekbones and then the soft bow-shaped curves of her lips "—it wasn't my feelings for them that kept me awake all last night." His thumbs drifted lower to her chin. "It was you, and this...." He dipped his head and delivered another hot, stirring kiss. It didn't last long but there was no denying the evidence of her own arousal or the immediacy of his response. He wanted her with a fierceness and tenderness that was both exciting and alarming, and she wanted him in exactly the same way.

Grace was trembling, weak-kneed and aching, when he let her go. The sinewy rigidity of his torso, and lower still, the pulsing heat, indicated he, too, was reluctant to part.

"Think about what I said, Grace," he said softly. His eyes searing into hers. "Think about what's going to happen after you leave here."

The answer came swiftly. She wanted him—and more. Much more. The question was, did he?

And if he didn't, would she be content with anything less than love, marriage and the whole commitment thing?

Grace had no answer for that. She only knew she had never wanted to live only in the moment as much as she did at that very second.

Outside, there was a burst of laughter and some gleeful, havoc-wreacking screams. Their gazes meshed. Grace sighed. "To be that young again," she murmured. "That carefree."

Ryan's eyes glimmered with wry amusement. "Believe me, I know." He grabbed his coat from the hook by the back door and paused to cast a look out the window. He grinned at the snow-throwing antics of the girls. "I better go supervise."

They'd like that, Grace knew. She nodded agreeably, springing into action, too. "I'll clean up here, get dressed and be right out to help."

"Take your time." He flashed her a winning smile as he buttoned up his coat and inched on his gloves. He looked back at the heaping mounds of snow and slowly shook his head. "Unless I miss my guess, this is going to take a while."

"WHY DON'T WE JUST wait for the snow to melt?" Hannah asked Ryan as they contemplated the task ahead.

Because that could be days from now, Ryan thought worriedly as he glanced in the direction of the Hindale farm, *and I may not have days to get all of you out of here.*

"We've only got two snow shovels, anyway," Greta indicated.

And only two girls old enough to be of any real help in the shoveling, Ryan thought, as he studied the long distance from the barn, where Grace's truck was parked, to the as-yet-unplowed road.

"And we wanted to go s-s-sledding today and build s-s-snowmen!" Letticia said.

"I can get a third shovel from the barn," Ryan suggested absently. It was meant for gardening and planting trees, but what the heck, it would work.

"It'll still take days!" Polly predicted as she stifled another sneeze.

"Not necessarily." As his next idea hit, Ryan grinned. "Not if we make the most of our resources and plan this out wisely."

Fifteen minutes later Ryan had them all busy. The two oldest girls, Darlene and Hannah, were helping him shovel two deep trenches, one for each side of the truck's wheels, through the snow from the barn clear down to the road. Meanwhile, the other five girls were making snowmen out of the snow in the middle of the two trenches, which further reduced the snow that had to be shoveled. They erected their various snowmen to the right of the semicleared drive. Everyone was happy and busy, it seemed, but Letticia, who—after only fifteen minutes of playing—had retreated to the front porch steps.

Noticing she had a particularly pouty expression on

her face and tears welling in her eyes, Ryan stopped what he was doing and went to tend to her. "What's the matter, Letticia?" Ryan asked gently as he got down on one knee in front of the six-year-old student.

"I can't d-d-do anything right," Letticia cried.

"Hey now," Ryan soothed. He pointed at the lop-sided snowman she'd been laboring over. "That's a very good snowman."

"But everyone else's is b-b-bigger and rounded. Mine is all l-l-lumpy and I can't even get it to stay together."

Realizing some tender loving care was called for, pronto, Ryan sat down on the top set and sat her on his knee. He'd had similar experiences when he was a kid, and knew how tough it was, feeling inadequate. "It's hard being the youngest, isn't it?" Ryan soothed gently as he laced a comforting arm about her tiny shoulders.

Too choked up to speak, Letticia nodded, tears rolling down her cheeks.

"You want to know how I know that?" Ryan continued, aware that this half-teaching, half-parenting business wasn't nearly as hard as it was cracked up to be.

Her lower lip quivering, Letticia regarded him solemnly.

"I know it 'cause I was the youngest, too. I had six brothers, and they were all older and bigger than me," Ryan said as he took off his glove and wiped the tears off her face. Remembering, he shook his head and let out a long, heartfelt sigh. "Let me tell you, they used to tease me something fierce."

Letticia took comfort in their shared problem. "Sometimes the other girls t-t-tease me, too," she told him.

Ryan nodded solemnly as he related, "It's pretty much the same way everywhere for us littlest ones. That's why you have to learn how to shrug it off and not care what they say and just go on being you."

"But that's jus' the p-p-problem, Ryan!" Letticia wailed upset. "I don't want to be me!"

Ryan blinked. "Why not?"

Letticia folded her arms in front of her adamantly. "'Cause I'm not s-s-special, like everyone else! I can't paint or s-s-sing or dance or do gymnastics or w-w-write stories."

"And other girls can, I take it?"

Keeping her arms locked in front of her tightly, Letticia nodded. "Everybody can do something n-n-neat to show off except me," she revealed sadly.

Ryan frowned thoughtfully. "I can see where that would be a problem." He ruffled her bangs. "Makes you feel bad, doesn't it?"

Letticia nodded, beginning to tear up again. "R-r-real bad."

"I know." Ryan sighed and commiserated gently, "I had the same problem when I was a kid. It seemed like no matter what I did—played sports or acted in the school play or played trumpet in the band—one of my brothers had not only already done it, they'd done it better than I ever could. And that made me real sad, 'cause I wanted to be best at something.''

Letticia took a moment to think about that. "So what'd you d-d-do?''

Ryan grinned. "Well, first off, I told myself I could be happy or sad, it was my choice. And I chose to be happy and put a smile on my face. Like this, see?'' Demonstrating, Ryan placed thumb and index finger at each corner of his comically scowling lips, and pushed the corners up into a goofy smile that made Letticia giggle.

"And then I decided that whatever I did decide to do, I was going to have fun doing it,'' Ryan told her firmly. "Maybe I wouldn't be the best or the first, but that didn't mean I couldn't do my own thing and have fun at the same time, so that's what I do.''

Letticia looked back out at the yard. "You mean I should m-m-make a snowman no matter *what* it looks like?''

"Letticia,'' Ryan said, nodding gravely, "that is exactly what I mean. 'Cause we only get one life, see, and we shouldn't waste it feeling sorry for ourselves or sad about what hasn't happened or might never happen and so on. We just need to get out there and do our best and have a good time.'' He lifted her off his lap and set her gently on the ground. "Now, do you think you can do that?''

Looking ready for action, Letticia nodded.

"Want my help?'' Ryan asked.

"No. I think if it's going to be d-d-dorky, I should do it all myself, but th-th-thanks, anyway, Ryan.''

Ryan grinned and gently tweaked her nose. "You bet."

He watched her rush back to her friends. Stood. And just then became aware he was not as alone as he'd thought.

"That was very nice, what you did for Letticia just now," Grace said softly.

Ryan turned. Grace was leaning against the side of the house. As their eyes met, she straightened and strolled toward him.

"You heard?" Ryan asked, feeling the tug of her presence like a lock on his heart. To his surprise, she'd left her hair down. She'd brushed it until it shone, and it fell like spun gold over her shoulders. As she neared him, the color heightened in her cheeks.

Her soft lips curved in a gentle smile. "I didn't mean to eavesdrop, but I was afraid if I moved in either direction I'd spoil the moment." She paused and their eyes locked. He felt the tug of the secrets they'd shared bringing them closer yet, and the warmth that flowed through him whenever she was near increased.

"You were very good with her," Grace continued, regarding him with praise-filled eyes as she shoved her gloved hands deep into the pockets of her coat.

The glove he'd taken off so he could wipe Letticia's tears still in his hand, Ryan shrugged and tried not to make too much of it. "I feel for her," he said simply.

"Because of your brothers," she guessed.

Ryan stepped a little closer, aware there was magic in the air this morning and it was all due to her. "Yeah." *Damn, but her eyes were a pretty shade of green. And her lips—had he ever seen any that were more kissable—more sweetly giving?*

She lifted her head slightly toward him. "Was it true, what you said to Letticia?" she asked softly, her face shining with a radiant light.

"Oh, yeah." Ryan traced her profile with the fingertips of his ungloved hand. "I was the last in a long line of superachievers, and it wasn't easy following in any of their footsteps."

"But you seem to have succeeded."

"With a lot of attitude," Ryan agreed. Aware that she'd not only left her hair down—for him, because he liked it that way, maybe?—but put on perfume, too, Ryan edged closer yet.

"And heart," Grace added, as she leaned into his touch. She told him happily, "You're gonna make a terrific dad some day."

Ryan dropped his hand from Grace's face and cast a look at the girls, who were, for the moment, anyway, wrapped up in their own activities. This was not a discussion he wanted to have here and now—the timing was all wrong. Since Grace had brought it up, however, he knew he owed it to her to be honest with her, even if she didn't like what he had to say.

"Considering what I do for a living, that's not all that likely."

"Because of the undercover work, and the danger."

Ryan nodded. "It'd be hard to have a family if you never saw them."

Having heard what Grace had been through, first with her parents who'd shipped her off to boarding school at an early age, and then her fiancé whose dedication to his work had cost them their chance to be married and be together as man and wife, he wasn't about to put Grace through that.

Some of the light went out of Grace's eyes. "Couldn't you do something else?"

If only it were that simple, Ryan thought. "I have done something else. I co-oped as an electrical engineer during college. It was a good job. An excellent company. And I hated every nine-to-five minute of it." So much so that he knew he couldn't go back, not even for Grace.

"Something else then?"

Ryan recalled the arduous years he'd spent struggling to figure out who he was, and the soul-deep relief he'd felt when he'd figured out where he belonged in the scheme of things. The Bureau was more than his job. It had become his home, his family, his whole life.

"Maybe at the Bureau?"

Ryan sighed. He knew there were boundless opportunities for analysts at the Bureau, but that was not where he belonged, either. "I'm not cut out for any kind of desk job, Grace." Knowing he was hurting her, but determined to be truthful anyway, Ryan swallowed.

This was dangerous territory. He had to be careful not to do anything to jeopardize the passion they felt for each other, or the once-in-a-lifetime love affair he was sure they were destined to have.

His tone lowered a compassionate notch as he took

one of her gloved hands in his. "This is my niche, Grace. It took me a long time to find it. I'm not sure I could give it up even if I wanted to do so. And frankly—I don't."

Ryan's words had not been meant to hurt her, but they had. She'd finally found a man who appealed to her on almost every level, and he was as married to his dangerous career as her former fiancé had been. When it came to her and romance, it seemed there was just no winning. And Grace couldn't help but wonder, as she and the girls helped Ryan clear the driveway all the way down to the road, if she'd ever get married or have the family of her own she so dearly wanted.

She knew with a certainty as solid as gold that the possibility of a sizzling love affair with Ryan was there for her to follow up on, once they'd left the farm and they were all out of danger. And while that was something she was still not inclined to pass up, even knowing all she did, she wondered if it would ever be enough. Would her memories of the love they'd shared be enough to sustain her through the lonely times ahead? Or would she, as she half expected, end up feeling angry and cheated when all was said and done?

Grace continued to ruminate on all the possibilities up to the time they'd finished shoveling snow at lunchtime. Ryan went off to the barn to check on her car and put the shovels away. Grace and her charges trooped back inside to warm up.

While soup simmered on the stove and the girls helped fix sandwiches and set the table, Grace called the headmistress to give her a progress report. "Well?" the girls demanded anxiously, when Grace'd hung up. "What'd she say?"

Exactly what I thought, Grace thought with a mixture of elation and dread. Grace smiled. "That we should stay put until we are absolutely certain it is safe to travel again. And the highway patrol says that won't be for at least another day or two."

A cheer went up around her. "Hurrah!"

"That means we get to stay with Ryan!"

"I like it here!"

"So do I!"

The problem was, Grace considered wryly, so did she. Maybe too much. If she wasn't careful, she could fall irrevocably in love with Ryan McCoy. And that could be disastrous, because right now—the undeniable pull between them aside—he was guarding his own heart as zealously as she was guarding hers.

Several minutes later Ryan came in the back door. His cheeks and nose were red with the cold. His hair was wind-tossed, and his face still bore a day's growth of beard. He looked sexy and rumpled in an irresistible sort of way. Even knowing what she did about their lack of a future together, it was all Grace could do not to go to him, take him in her arms and welcome him home like the defending warrior he was.

"Where were you?" the girls demanded all at once as he shrugged out of his coat and took off his snow-covered boots.

"Yeah," Greta added, "we looked outside a couple of times and we couldn't see you at all."

Grace looked at Ryan's aw-shucks expression and knew where he'd really been just now: the cave, checking on the goings-on at the Hindale farm.

Ryan grinned and raked a hand casually through his hair. "Oh, I was out and about, taking a look at the snow." Ryan edged closer to Grace and the stove. He rubbed his hands together vigorously to warm them. "I hate to tell you but it looks like there's a whole new batch of winter storm clouds coming in from the south."

The youthful faces surrounding him looked both elated and alarmed. "You think it's going to snow again?" Hannah asked.

"Maybe," Ryan said. He tilted his head in the direction of the other room. "Let's go check the weather channel."

Together they trooped into the living room and switched on the TV. Sure enough, Grace noted with dismay, there was another front moving in, fast on the heels of the first. "With snow, up to six inches in the mountains, starting late this evening..." the announcer said.

The girls cheered while Ryan and Grace exchanged fearful looks. Grace was relieved she and Ryan didn't have to part company just yet but was worried that she and the girls were still in danger, and would be, until they got completely away from Hindale and his gun-loving friends across the valley. Nevertheless she took comfort in the rugged terrain and woods that separated the two farms, and obscured them from view.

"Does this mean we won't be able to leave tomorrow after all?" one of the girls asked.

Grace looked at Ryan, and the silence seemed to last an eternity.

"It just might," Ryan said eventually. The smile he gave the girls did not quite reach his eyes. "We'll have to wait and see."

Grace knew what he was thinking. He was worried about keeping them safe. So was she. But she couldn't discuss any of that in front of the children. She would have to get Ryan alone to discover if he thought Hindale et al might act before then.

She gave Ryan an officious smile. "Lunch won't be ready for another fifteen minutes. I think I'll bring some more wood up to the porch."

"I'll help you."

The girls made a "whoo" sound, giggled softly and exchanged knowing looks.

"I think they're in love!" Clara sang out, and the girls giggled all the harder.

Grace rolled her eyes in exasperation. Ryan mugged comically. Once again, they grabbed their coats, hats, gloves and boots and headed out. As soon as they were away from the house, Grace asked, "So what did you see at the cave?" she asked, turning up her collar against the brisk winter wind.

Ryan sighed and squinted into the horizon as they stomped toward the woodpile next to the barn. "They don't just have one tank over there, they have two. Plus ten more foot soldiers than I knew about." Fortunately, the limited surveillance capabilities the militia possessed were all directed at their target.

Grace tensed inwardly at the news. "Bringing the total to..."

Ryan clamped his lips together grimly. "Twenty."

Heavily armed men and women... "You're worried," Grace said. *As am I.*

His easygoing demeanor dropping, Ryan nodded in the affirmative. "And frustrated," he said, as he looked at her, "because at this moment I have no way to get you and the girls out of here without drawing attention to ourselves. We have to put this militia group out of business before they hurt someone, and we won't be able to do that if they split up before we can get agents with warrants in."

Grace bent to the pile and carefully gathered up an armload of wood. "Maybe it won't snow again tonight."

"Maybe not," Ryan agreed grimly, but he did not look encouraged as he, too, picked up a load. "In any case, there will be no police action on the part of the Bureau until I can get you and the girls out of here."

Grace sighed her relief. "Thank you. I appreciate that."

"No problem."

They turned, firewood cradled in their arms, to see seven faces pressed up against the back windows. Caught spying, the girls all jumped back and pretended not to have seen. Watching, Ryan laughed and shook his head. "Those kids won't give up, will they?"

"Nope. They want us to have a romance."

"And what about you, Grace? What do you want?"

Grace released a soft, wistful breath. He'd been honest with her. She owed it to him to be honest about her feelings, too. She pursed her lips together ruefully. "I wish we'd met some other time, some other way."

Ryan wished they'd met some other place, some other way, too. Because if they had, he would've chased Grace until she surrendered. Even with things the way they were, he didn't want her to leave until she absolutely had to leave. Yet there was no way he was going to risk them being taken hostage, either. And that meant he had to get them out of there as soon as possible. Or as soon as the roads were cleared. In the meantime, it was best to keep everyone calm and pleasantly occupied. He didn't want Grace dwelling on any plans Hindale might have. If she were worried, the girls would pick up on it.

"So what's on your agenda for this afternoon?" Ryan asked Grace casually as they again started for the farmhouse.

Grace took the steps and dumped the snow-covered firewood on top of the dwindling pile next to the back door. "The girls mentioned they saw a couple of old sleds hanging up on the wall of the barn."

"Yeah." Ryan set his firewood on top of hers. He straightened. "They were left here by the previous owner."

Grace tilted her face up to his. Her breath formed rings in the air between them. "Would it be all right if I let them go sledding on the hill behind the farm-house?''

The hill could not be seen from the Hindale farm, and with the roads between here and there impassable, Ryan saw no harm in it. In fact, it'd probably be a good way to keep them all busy. ''Sure. The sleds need to be cleaned up a little first, but I can help with that.''

She stepped back and surveyed him from head to toe. ''You wouldn't mind?''

Ryan continued to delay going in, where young ears eagerly deciphered every word they said. ''Haven't you figured it out yet?'' he replied softly, knowing that as odd as it was, as unexpected, he meant the words with all his heart. ''There isn't anything I wouldn't do to help keep you safe and happy.''

Chapter Nine

"It's too scary," Brianna announced. "I can't do it."

Grace looked at the next-to-youngest student in her group and knew she'd be missing out on a lot of hilarity if she didn't. Plus, the group activity would be a good panacea for the homesickness Brianna—the newest Peach Blossom student—had been feeling.

She knelt down in front of her, so they were at eye level. "Brianna, honey, it's fun. I promise." Furthermore, Grace knew if Brianna just sledded down the hill once, she'd be hooked.

"No way!" Brianna crossed her arms in front of her stubbornly and looked up to the top of the snow-covered hill.

And Grace suddenly knew trying to talk her into trying this was a lost cause. The painfully shy seven-year-old had been a good sport so far, weathering the snowstorm and their makeshift accommodations with alacrity, but she was clearly drawing the line at this.

Brianna stared at the top of the long, gently sloping hill and shook her head, frightened at just the thought. "I'm *not* going up there."

The faces of the other girls mirrored Grace's private disappointment as Grace and Ryan traded glances over Brianna's head.

"I'll sit on the sled with you," fourteen-year-old Hannah offered with her customary good cheer.

"No!" Brianna stuck her thumb in her mouth, insulated mitten and all.

"You go on up and supervise the other girls. I'll stay here and hang out with Brianna," Ryan offered. "We've got a good view of all the goings-on, right, Brianna?" Ryan smiled at Grace. "We don't mind just watching."

Brianna sent Ryan a grateful look and tucked her mittened hand into his. "Yeah, we don't mind just watching," she parroted.

"Okay," Grace said, aware the other girls were getting restless. *Maybe Ryan would work the same magic on Brianna he had on Letticia a while ago.* She patted Brianna's shoulder. "Just remember—you can come up and join us anytime, if you do change your mind."

Grace led the girls to the top of the hill. Quickly they reviewed the ground rules and got to it. The girls took turns sledding, two at a time, whooping it up gleefully as they went. Brianna watched enviously from the bottom for a good twenty minutes.

Grace saw Ryan talk to Brianna some more.

Then, to everyone's amazement, Brianna took a turn all by herself—sledding not from the top of the hill, but about six feet from the bottom. Then ten feet, twelve, fifteen, and finally, all the way to the top.

"Did you see me, Ms. Tennessen?" Brianna asked

excitedly, running up to join her, Ryan not far behind. "I did it! I really did it!"

"That's great, Brianna." Grace knelt to give her a congratulatory hug.

"Ryan taught me how!" Brianna announced breathlessly, looking happier—and more a part of the group—than she had since she'd been sent to boarding school.

Grace grinned. "I can see that. He's a fabulous teacher, isn't he?"

Brianna nodded and, her face still glowing, ran off to play. Grace dusted off her knees and got up. "I haven't seen you sledding," Ryan teased.

Grace returned his half smile. "You, neither."

He stared at her, fascinated. "Want to try?"

Her smile blossomed in an instant. "You're kidding, right?" Grace touched a self-conscious hand to her hair.

He shook his head. Leaning closer, he chided, his warm breath ghosting past her cheek, "Even teachers are allowed to have a little fun."

"Yeah, Ms. Tennessen! Try it!" the girls encouraged as they picked up on the activity and gathered round.

Ryan lifted a brow, silently daring Grace to give it a try. "I will if you will!" he said.

A little thrill of excitement—and something else—raced through her. "Why not?" Grace drawled, aware he was making her feel like a kid again and that it felt good to be doing something purely for pleasure's sake.

Together, they strode up the hill. She climbed on a sled. Ryan climbed on right behind her.

"I thought you were going to take the other one," she protested breathlessly, as he hooked his long legs alongside her and wrapped his arms around her.

He pulled her back against the hardness of his chest. "I think we can both fit on this one. Ready?" His warm breath tickled her neck as she relaxed against him involuntarily.

"As I'll ever be," Grace acknowledged breathlessly.

He pushed off with his feet. The next thing Grace knew the wind was in their faces and they were flying over the top of the hill and bumping recklessly down the long, gentle slope. The girls cheered behind them as the sled's momentum slowed and then finally stopped. Disappointed to find the wild ride over so soon—she had liked having the wind in her face and being held against his solid chest that way—Grace waited for Ryan to disembark first. "Cool, huh?" he said, gallantly taking her hand in his and helping her to her feet.

Grace grinned and borrowed a term from her kids. "Way cool, actually." She'd like to do it again and again, she thought, as their eyes met and held.

And suddenly above them, all went silent on the hill. In unison, Grace and Ryan turned. Ryan sucked in his breath. The hair on the back of Grace's neck stood on end. There, beside the girls was Ryan's dangerous neighbor, Hindale, and another man. Both were dressed in military combat fatigues and heavy black boots. They had bright orange hunting vests and hats on, and lethal-looking rifles slung over their shoulders.

"Hey, neighbor!" Hindale waved.

Ryan nodded his head in acknowledgment. He reached over to take Grace's hand and squeezed it reassuringly, until she felt his protection like a shield of armor.

"Hey there," Ryan drawled with a kindly smile as he let go of Grace's hand and walked toward Hindale.

Hindale returned Ryan's grin with one of his own. "We heard all the noise over here, so Hal and I came across the valley to see what was going on. You didn't say anything about having kids with you."

Ryan shrugged matter-of-factly at the oversight and replied with a calm Grace found remarkable. "Grace is a schoolteacher. She had her students with her on a field trip when she stopped by. Guess they were already in the farmhouse when you ran into us on the road."

Hindale paused a moment to take that in while his partner, a husky man in his late forties, leered at Grace. "Lucky you had a flat tire here then, isn't it?" Hindale said, zeroing in on the bizarre coincidence that had landed Grace in Ryan's arms.

"You're right," Grace smiled as she struggled to contain an involuntary shudder. She stepped forward, putting herself and Ryan between Hindale and his crony and the girls. "It could have been so much worse," Grace continued pleasantly. She could have ended up going to the Hindale farm for help.

"So when's the big day?" Hindale asked, studying

their faces. "When are you and McCoy getting hitched?"

"Hitched!" Hannah repeated dumbly, as if she were sure she hadn't heard right.

"You know—married," Hindale replied before Grace or Ryan could get a word in edgewise.

And then it was too late. All around them, the girls mouths dropped open in surprise. Then the reactions came fast and furious as everyone spoke at once.

"You're really getting married, Miss Tennessen?"

"See, I told you they were in love!"

"This is so cool!"

"Not to mention romantic!"

"Girls," Grace interjected in her most-prim schoolteacher tone. "I'm sure these two gentlemen aren't interested in my relationship with Mr. McCoy.

"On the contrary." Hindale frowned. He peered at Grace suspiciously. "How come your students didn't know you two were engaged?"

Grace looked Hindale straight in the eye. "I wanted them to get to know and like Ryan *before* we told them we were romantically involved."

"When are you getting married?" Hindale asked.

Ryan stepped back to close the distance between himself and Grace. Smiling, he linked his arm around Grace's waist. "As soon as I can get her to set a date," he admitted possessively, pressing a kiss to her forehead.

At Ryan's matter-of-fact announcement, a whoop of utter delight went up from the girls. They hugged each other and jumped up and down. "We want to be part of the wedding, too, Miss Tennessen!" Clara declared.

Grace smiled, and she tightened her hand in Ryan's as her heart continued to pound. "Not to worry, girls. I'll see you're included in everything that happens."

"Yeah, maybe Ryan can even write a song about it," Polly suggested.

Ryan smiled. "That's a good idea. I'll give it a try."

Hindale rubbed his jaw. "Say, you wouldn't mind if my buddy and I popped into your kitchen a moment and got a drink of water, would you?" Hindale asked. He opened the canteen he was carrying and tipped it upside down. "It's bone-dry."

Oh, dear heavens, Grace thought as Ryan smiled and said gregariously, "No problem. Just help yourself."

"Thanks." Hindale and his friend headed for the farmhouse.

Wondering what Hindale was up to now, Grace and Ryan watched the two men disappear inside.

"You girls can go back to sledding," Ryan told them.

"We wanted to talk about the wedding."

"We will later," Grace promised.

Satisfied, the girls raced off with the sleds in tow.

"So what's going on?" Grace asked Ryan, the moment they were out of earshot of the girls.

"Can't tell you." Ryan pushed the words through his teeth. "But I imagine we'll find out shortly," he predicted grimly.

"And for the moment?"

"Just pretend absolutely nothing's wrong." Ryan smiled and waved and shouted encouragement at the girls while Grace obediently followed suit.

A tense three minutes later, Hindale and his friend emerged from the back door of Ryan's farmhouse. As they waved and went on their way, a light, dry snow began to fall. "We better get the girls back to the farmhouse," Ryan said quietly, the moment the coast was clear.

"Right."

"When we get there, I want you to busy them outside for a moment while I do a sweep of the house," Ryan announced irritably. "Wait until I give you a signal before you bring any of them inside."

Which meant what? Grace thought, her heart beginning to thud. She swallowed hard as she tilted her face up to his. "You don't think—?"

"That they'd harm us now? No," Ryan interjected firmly, "I don't. But they were clearly up to something," he told her grimly, his golden-brown eyes narrowing, "and I want to know what."

Grace gathered up the girls, aware—even if they weren't—that the sweet mountain air now seemed charged with danger. They put the sleds back in the barn and paused to lug some extra firewood up to the back porch and discuss the new snow falling, while Ryan went on inside.

By the time they'd finished, Ryan gestured them in. Again he smiled at her. "Have the girls showered today?" he asked Grace.

She shook her head.

"Maybe now would be the time for that," he said.

She caught the silent message in his eyes. He wanted them busy so the two of them could talk.

Grace grinned at her charges, as if it were just another day in a rather mundane life, and said dryly, "Girls, you heard the man. Now's the time to empty the hot water tank, so you-all get started on that while Ryan and I figure out what we're going to have for dinner."

To Grace's chagrin, her announcement was followed by a burst of giggles and sly grins. "I think they want to be alone," Polly said.

"Yeah," Hannah agreed. "And why not, since they're secretly engaged?"

More giggles followed and then the girls trooped out and bounded up the stairs.

The moment they were gone, Ryan took Grace in his arms, "Alone at last!" he murmured theatrically. His golden-brown eyes glimmering with a message Grace couldn't begin to decipher, he said wickedly, "Come here, darlin', and give me a kiss!"

A kiss! Now? Was he nuts? Grace thought.

But when she would've protested out loud, he gave her a look and placed a silencing finger against her lips.

Taking her gently by the hand, he tiptoed with her over to one of the kitchen cabinets, and situated the two of them right next to it.

"Mmm, honey, you feel so good," he moaned softly but distinctly. To Grace's chagrin, he sounded as though he was in the midst of one hot necking session.

Still holding a finger to his lips, he pointed beneath the cabinet. "Yeah, like that, honey, just like that," Ryan continued, moaning and breathing heavily, as Grace bent and looked beneath the cabinet.

For the second time in as many minutes her mouth opened in surprise. Her glance cut back to his. "Is that a bug?" she mouthed. If so, it was the first time she had ever seen a listening device in real life.

Ryan nodded affirmatively and leaned closer to the bug.

He rubbed the sleeve of his shirt against the sleeve of hers, until it made a rustling sound. "Oh, honey, c'mon, let's go up to the bedroom," he murmured, undoubtedly for the benefit of those on the other end of the listening device.

Grace wasn't sure how far he intended to go with this farce. Nor was she sure she wanted to find out.

"The girls!" Grace protested, just as succinctly.

Ryan grinned stubbornly and moaned again, soft and low, in a sound that was so authentic and full of desire that it had her insides melting.

"Won't miss us if we disappear for five or ten or even fifteen minutes," he encouraged slyly.

"Ryan—" Grace chided, shocked as the melting sensation inside her deepened all the more, and the color in her cheeks increased. "C'mon...you're not being fair."

"Unfair is depriving me of your love," Ryan said,

even more firmly. "Now, kiss me baby," he drawled in that soft, honeyed Southern voice of his.

His eyes still on hers, he inclined his head in the direction of the stairs. He took her hand in his and they went upstairs soundlessly.

They looked in on the girls, who were playing a game of Go Fish as they waited their turns for the shower. Then Ryan tugged her into the master bedroom. He shut the door behind them.

"Ryan!" Grace exclaimed, beginning to get even more flustered. "I really must complain—"

Ryan pointed to a painting of Willie Nelson he'd hung on the wall above his bureau. Underneath the frame was another bug.

"Complain all you want," Ryan said firmly, continuing the audio drama he'd started downstairs, "we're still going to make love."

Like heck they were, Grace thought as she flattened a hand against his chest. "Not until we're married, we're not," she said firmly, keeping her voice just loud enough for the listening device to pick it up. "I have an example to set for my girls."

Ryan's eyes gleamed with rich amusement as he silently applauded her performance. At last she was giving him exactly what he wanted. "And I told you, honey, I *can't* marry you until you set a date, and you said you wouldn't do that until I become a country-singing success."

"That could take years!" Grace complained in mock feminine outrage.

"Exactly. Which is why I want us to make love

now, instead of later. Besides, think of the inspiration you'll be providing me, honey. This'll make a great country song. Heck, it might even be my first hit.'' He hummed a few notes, then sang in true hillbilly fashion, ''The snow was coming down from the sky...when what should happen but my true love came by...she had a flat tire on her truck now...and a carload of little girls...but that don't matter, no it don't...'cause we was in lo-o-o-ve with each other, yes we were—''

Ryan stopped abruptly as Grace clamped both hands over her mouth to smother a giggle. She couldn't help it, his singing was just so bad!

He mock-scowled at her. ''Well, that's all I've got so far,'' he said, aiming his lazy voice in the direction of the bug, ''but you can see the song's coming along.''

As was his new approach here, she thought.

''Then finish the song,'' Grace told him, electing to pretend to be as difficult with him as he was pretending to be with her.

''Oh, honey,'' Ryan pleaded, for the benefit of the listening device. ''C'mon,'' he said, surprising her and drawing her into his arms once again. ''Just one kiss,'' he murmured, as his mouth lowered to hers and he gazed deep into her eyes. ''One itty...bitty...kiss....''

Heat moved slowly through her body, a soft moan escaped her throat, and then his mouth was on hers. Touching and enticing, flooding her with sensations and a soft, melting need that went soul deep. Unable to resist, Grace pressed her breasts against the warmth of his chest and opened her lips to his. Ryan murmured his pleasure as their tongues twined together, their hearts beat as one and the kiss turned into a second and a third.

Before she knew it, she was forgetting all about the tiny microphone and kissing him back, magically, passionately. His hands were sliding down her back, to the small of her spine. Pressing her against him, he let her feel the sheer implacability of his passion. He made her feel beautiful and desirable. And as he did, Grace realized the unthinkable was happening.

It might not be wise, she might not want to admit it, but the truth was she was falling in love with Ryan. And more importantly still, she wanted to make love with him. And though he'd been scrupulously honest in pointing out to her that the nature of his work kept him from seeking a lasting commitment with any woman, she also knew how rare chemistry like theirs was.

This might be the last—the only—chance she ever had to experience the physical side of love, in a truly wondrous and satisfying manner. She didn't want to blow that opportunity, she thought, by waiting too long the way she did the last time.

But to do otherwise—

Grace moaned in giddy, conflicted pleasure, not sure she could sacrifice principles for pleasure, no matter how much she wanted and loved him. Should she love him now and risk all? Or wait and risk that it might never happen at all?

For several more minutes Ryan continued to kiss

her with a hunger and desperation she not only understood but felt, too. Finishing, Ryan let her go. As she looked into his eyes, she knew he was suffering the same quandary. Life wasn't simple. Neither was this. Life didn't come without consequences. Neither would this. And yet, some pleasures...some opportunities were worth the risk.

At least that's what she thought he was thinking until he said, in true cad fashion, "See how much inspiration you provide me with?"

Grace rolled her eyes. Had this all been part of the ruse? Or was it as real as she'd thought? "Listen up, Ryan McCoy!" she told him hotly, even as she wondered who-all besides Hindale and his friend were listening to this staged lover's quarrel. "You may have thought that kiss was cute—" she said as she shook a finger at him.

"Sexy, is how I'd categorize it," Ryan interrupted.

"But any further inspiration you get will come *after* I get a ring on my finger, and not before," she told him loudly.

Ryan grinned, obviously delighted at the way she was playing along with him. "Now, Grace, honey," he drawled, in country boy fashion, "don't be mad—"

"Too late, Ryan," Grace said hotly, aware even as she spoke that it was true. "I already am." And she had every right to be! She couldn't tell when Ryan was playing a role with her, and when he was being serious. She only knew that when he got romantic, it felt real. And that she couldn't begin to switch gears as easily or swiftly as he could.

Ryan caught her arm before she could pivot away from him. "Now, Grace," he scolded softly, still aiming his voice in the direction of the tiny microphone. "Don't go storming off before we have a chance to—"

"Kiss again?" Grace interrupted haughtily, jerking free. "I don't think so." She aimed her voice at the picture frame, too. "Besides, I think I hear the girls calling me," she fibbed. "I've got to go."

Ryan nodded in agreement and pointed wordlessly toward the first floor, indicating he wanted to meet her there. "All right, but we're not finished with this discussion yet," he said loudly.

Grace folded her arms in front of her. "You know my terms," she reminded defiantly.

"That I do."

Grace spun on her heel and swiftly opened the door. The moment she did so, seven little girls ended up in a heap.

Grace stared at them as they all scrambled to their feet. "You all were eavesdropping?"

One and all looked hideously embarrassed. "Sorry, Ms. Tennessen," Hannah said promptly.

"We couldn't help it," Greta confessed.

"We wanted to know what was going on, and why you were tiptoeing around," Darlene said.

Polly scowled. "Miss Tennessen's right, you know, Ryan. You shouldn't try to, well—" she flushed bright red "—get her into bed before the two of you marry."

"Yeah, she deserves a commitment from you!" the group agreed in unison. *"And a ring."*

Feeling embarrassed beyond belief to be caught in such a sticky situation, yet all too aware they were still in danger, Grace drew a breath. Mindful of both her responsibility to the girls and the listening devices and the criminals on the other end of them, not sure there weren't any more tiny microphones hidden in the house, she looked at Ryan for a clue what to do next. He, too, was upset by the turn of events. Apparently as much by the bad example they'd just set as by the risks inherent in the situation.

"You're right, girls," Ryan said solemnly to one and all as he wrapped a possessive arm about her waist. "I have been unfair, not just to your teacher, but to all of you, as well. And there is only one solution to this."

Grace looked at Ryan, knowing him too well to be reassured by the twinkle in his golden-brown eyes and the determined expression on his face. "And that would be what?" she croaked nervously.

Ryan sobered. "You've got to marry me, Grace. The sooner, the better."

Chapter Ten

Grace laughed nervously. "I thought that was already decided. I am, after all, your secret—" *at least as far as the girls are concerned* "—fiancée."

"And now that everyone knows," Ryan inclined his head ever so slightly toward the listening device planted in the bedroom, "I think we ought to get married now...tonight."

Grace tried to stifle a gasp and failed. "That's...that's impossible! It's snowing again and the roads are still unnavigable, and...and we have no minister or justice of the peace here!" Not to mention the fact a marriage, even a pretend one, would complicate their lives immensely!

Ryan shrugged, while the starry-eyed girls surrounding them hung on their every word, look and gesture. "Those are all obstacles that can be overcome," he told her confidently.

Grace could feel her knees quivering. "How?" she asked desperately, aware that this situation here—very much like her feelings for Ryan—kept getting more out of hand with every second that passed.

"I'll telephone the minister at the community church in town and see if he'll marry us by telephone."

Grace stared at him as though he'd gone mad. He wasn't just buying time; he was serious about getting this done and done quickly. "Come again?" she croaked nervously, aware she sounded—and felt—very much like a bride with a case of the pre-wedding jitters. And Ryan, like a man who'd been without his "woman" for far too long.

"Well, think about it," Ryan replied easily. There was a light in his eyes that hadn't been there before. "No minister or justice of the peace actually has to see us to take our vows, he or she just has to hear us recite them. And—" he turned to smile at the youthful faces surrounding them "—the girls here can act as witnesses."

Grace shook her head. "But there are licenses to consider and—"

"Mere paperwork, all of which can be cleared up afterward as soon as the weather clears. In the meantime," Ryan laid a hand against her cheek, "we'd be man and wife in every sense that counted. Think of it, Grace," he said softly, looking deep into her eyes. His voice was urgent with the need to make her understand. "If we do this, it'll solve so many problems."

Grace had only to look into Ryan's sexy eyes to know what he was thinking would be gained by such a frivolous action. Her reputation would be saved, the girls would not be privy to quite such a bad example, and best of all, Hindale and his felonious cronies would have no more reason to suspect that she and Ryan were anything but two people who were madly in love with each other.

And while Grace wanted all that, too, she still felt confused and off kilter by the quick and impulsive way all this had come about. She raked a hand through her hair. "I need a moment to think about this."

Ryan drew her all the way into his arms even as he looked at the young faces surrounding them. "Girls? Don't you have some showers to finish taking?"

"We're going, we're going," Greta said, as unhappy as the rest of the group to be banished from the unfolding drama in which nothing was quite settled yet.

"Say yes, Miss Tennessen!" Hannah urged, practically jumping up and down in her glee.

"Yeah, say yes!" the rest of the girls chimed in, as they too shared in the mounting excitement.

Still holding her close, Ryan took Grace's hand and gently kissed the back of it. "While you're thinking about it," he said, fixing her with a highly charged look that told her he saw no other way out of the predicament they found themselves in. "Let's go downstairs and get that fire roaring in the grate."

So they could be alone and he could kiss her again? Grace wondered, knowing full well that Ryan McCoy was not above using that highly effective form of persuasion, any more than she was above falling for it. Yet she also knew that the girls could not hear any more of the ensuing discussion. They'd already seen and heard far too much!

Grace promised the girls gently, "We'll call you when we're ready to start dinner."

Ryan winked. "Or in other words, stay upstairs until we call you." He chuckled as he gave Grace yet another unabashedly ardent look. "And this time no peeking or eavesdropping!"

At his last instruction, more giggles abounded but they went off to do as asked, and Ryan and Grace went downstairs to the living room.

Once there, Ryan took Grace by the hand and pointed out yet another electronic listening device attached to the bottom of the hurricane lamp on the mantel.

"Want some help with the fire?" Grace asked, in as normal a tone as possible.

"Thanks, sweetheart, I can handle it." He winked at her and said ardently, "You just get yourself in the mood for some lovin'."

Grace rolled her eyes even as her pulse upped another notch. "I haven't said yes yet!" she reminded.

"You will," Ryan promised in a low, sexy voice, also looking less than enthused. As if, she thought, he had some reservations of his own about all this, too. But was bent on this course of action, nonetheless.

Grace fell silent, watching Ryan work. Minutes later, he had the fire blazing and the stereo crooning soft, romantic Willie Nelson ballads. Finished, he straightened and held out his arms to her. "I'm ready if you are," he announced.

Wondering what he was up to now, Grace gave him a quizzical look and situated herself next to the hurricane lamp on the mantel. She'd thought they were going to talk some more. Instead, he seemed to want to do everything but that. "You want to dance?" she asked curiously.

"Darlin', I always want to dance," Ryan told her sexily as he closed the distance between them in two swift strides and took her into his arms.

"Come closer," Ryan murmured into the hurricane lamp, for the benefit of those spying on them. "I want to hold all of you against all of me."

For her benefit alone, he then danced her away from the lamp and put his face next to hers and murmured, "I want to whisper in your ear."

The bugs— Grace mouthed in protest.

Ryan's arms tightened around her possessively. "Aren't powerful enough to pick up our whispers over the music, so say anything you want to me, hon, as long as you whisper in my ear."

"Okay." Grace placed her arms around his neck and stood on tiptoe to whisper as they swayed back and forth to the soft, seductive beat of the music. "This is nuts."

Ryan tightened his arms around her so that all of her was in contact with all of him. "I agree," he whispered back, as her slender body molded with his, and shivers of yearning swept through Grace.

"Why can't we just take the bugs out?"

Ryan quirked a brow and smiled an unbearably kind smile. "And immediately tip them off to the fact we're on to them?"

Grace sighed. Her face brushed the beard-roughened skin of his face as she whispered back, "Good point."

"I know it's nerve-racking," Ryan soothed, as he used the palms of both hands to warmly massage his way down her spine.

"No kidding," Grace lamented softly, as she rested her cheek against his jaw. "It feels like Big Brother is watching," she continued, her voice catching in her throat.

Ryan traced the shell of her ear with the pad of his thumb. "Which is exactly why we should get married," he told her assuredly.

"Tonight?" Grace asked, not sure how she felt about that. Nervous, that it was happening at all. Excited, that it should be happening now, tonight.

Ryan nodded as he gave her a fleeting yet tender kiss. "The sooner the better," he said.

If this would keep them safe, what choice did she have? Grace took a deep breath. "All right."

"YOU'RE REALLY GONNA do it?" the girls asked, when Ryan and Grace announced it to them half an hour later.

Grace nodded. It was a crazy tactic, but given the circumstances, also the only way she knew to throw Hindale and his cronies off Ryan's track and keep the girls safe. "We applied for the license by phone while you girls were finishing your showers, and Ryan arranged for the minister to call here at seven."

The marriage would only be legal if they passed their blood tests, which was, Grace figured, the technical way out of this later that Ryan was counting on. One or the other would either refuse to take the test or have an "unsatisfactory" result—which would mean the license was invalid, and so was the actual marriage.

"Seven tonight!" Darlene echoed in shock.

"Ohmygosh, that means we've only got an hour to get you ready!" Hannah cried to Grace in distress.

"What do you mean, 'get me ready'?" Grace asked warily, very much aware the listening devices were picking up every word of this discussion with the girls.

"You've got to wear a white dress," Polly insisted.

Grace grinned, knowing that was something easier said than done. "Small problem," she said, hating to have to disappoint the girls, who were clearly so thrilled to be witnessing her "marriage" to Ryan. "I don't have one with me."

The girls exchanged looks that begged to differ with that statement, but Polly was the one who finally spoke up. "What about that long frilly white gown and robe in your suitcase?"

Grace flushed despite herself as she caught the spark of amusement and delighted male interest in Ryan's golden eyes.

Trying not to feel panicked at the thought of what they were about to do, she said, "That's not a dress, it's a peignoir set!"

"So?" The girls shrugged in unison as Hannah continued acting as one of the spokespersons for the group. "You could wear them both, and belt the robe or something, and make it look like an old fashioned wedding dress, couldn't you?''

Grace took a deep, bracing breath. ''Well, I suppose I could if I were really desperate.'' She just wasn't sure she was that desperate yet.

''And you could wear it with those white satin bedroom slippers you have, instead of high heels,'' Clara pointed out.

Grace met Ryan's eyes. He nodded his head in the direction of the tiny microphone hidden beneath the hurricane lamp on the mantel of the fireplace. He was urging her to go for it—and in the process give Hindale and his buddies something to talk about all evening.

Grace looked back at the girls, who were supporting this idea as enthusiastically as Ryan.

She flushed self-consciously as half of Ryan's mouth lifted in a knowing grin. ''Oh, why not,'' she said dryly, unable and unwilling to disappoint the girls, who were so excited they could hardly stand it. After all, what harm could it do? She and Ryan knew this was all pretend. And in the meantime, all the activity would help pass the time. ''I'll see what I can do to transform the peignoir set into a wedding dress.''

Her announcement was met by cheers from the girls. ''And we'll make you a bouquet and everything,'' Hannah promised.

This promise had both Ryan and Grace perplexed. Grace blinked. ''Out of what?'' she asked.

The girls smiled mysteriously—obviously this was something they had already talked about and planned out in private. "Never you mind," Darlene said, waving off further questions.

"Just go get ready," Polly said.

"And I'll get ready, too," Ryan promised.

An hour later all was in readiness. Grace was upstairs. The girls were dressed in their Peach Blossom Academy uniforms. Soft music was playing on Ryan's stereo.

At Grace's insistence, the girls all served as her attendants.

At their insistence, Grace followed them down the stairs, with a bouquet of flowers, fashioned out of pastel-colored facial tissues, in her hands.

Ryan was standing by the fireplace.

He looked incredibly handsome in a pale green dress shirt and coordinating tie, moss green corduroy jacket and jeans. His soft glossy hair was combed to perfection, his face closely shaved and scented with aftershave. His golden-brown eyes were sparkling with life and fastened firmly on her as he extended a hand to her.

Her heart pounding, Grace meshed her fingers with his.

And that was when the phone rang.

"It's the minister from town, Reverend Smithey. He wants to know if you two're ready to tie the knot?" Hannah asked.

Ryan looked at Grace, so beautiful and ethereal in her gauzy white peignoir set, with her hair done up in a knot high atop her head. Wispy blond bangs brushed her forehead, and tendrils curled against the nape of her neck and the tops of her ears, and fell gently against her face. Pale pink color bloomed in her cheeks. Her eyes danced with an intoxicating blend of excitement and wariness.

Ryan said they were ready, aware he had never felt the kind of passion for anyone else that he felt for Grace. Unbeknownst to anyone else this was a pretend ceremony. But with Grace in front of him, looking like this, with him in a suit and tie, it was beginning to feel mighty real.

Which was yet another reason to simply get it over with, he thought.

"Push the speaker-box switch on the telephone and turn up the volume all the way," Ryan instructed.

Hannah, who was in charge of the combination phone and answering machine during the ceremony, swiftly did as directed.

"Can you hear me?" Reverend Smithey asked as his voice was broadcast throughout the room.

"Loud and clear," Ryan replied.

"All right then," Reverend Smithey replied, as the girls, who were almost beside themselves with excitement, too, grinned happily. "We'll get started.

"Grace, do you take Ryan to be your lawfully wedded husband?"

Grace swallowed hard as she clutched her bouquet with damp fingers. "I do."

"Ryan, do you take Grace to be your lawfully wedded wife?"

He looked at her solemnly, and replied, "I do."

"Then, by the power vested in me by the state of

Virginia, I now pronounce you man and wife. Ryan, you may kiss the bride.''

Aware her heart was pounding in her throat, and that Ryan was suddenly very, very close to her, Grace lifted her face and prepared herself for a quick, passionless peck on the lips. To her utter astonishment, Ryan took her all the way into his arms, and bent her backward from the waist. He clasped her to him and ever so slowly, ever so deliberately, threaded one hand through her hair and took her lips with the passion she had yearned to know again. Grace reveled in the hard, insistent demand of his mouth and the ardent sweep of his tongue. She melted against him, her hand curling around his shoulders.

She meant to resist him, but there was just something about the way his lips moved on hers—so provocatively and surely—that totally sapped her will. He was just so strong, so determined and so giving. He created within her a need unlike any she had ever known. And as their kiss came to a necessary halt, Grace had the feeling it was all he could do, too, to stop.

And then it was over.

The girls all screamed in excitement and clapped and hugged each other and Grace and Ryan deliriously.

Warmest congratulations were offered all around.

Grace looked at Ryan.

Ryan looked at Grace.

"Well," he concluded triumphantly, for the benefit of both Reverend Smithey and those on the other end of the listening device. "We're finally married, sweetheart."

Grace regarded Ryan as if she were unable to believe this was really happening to them. Ryan thought he even understood why. They might be married in the technical sense, at least for the moment, but he suspected Grace, like him, did not really feel the least bit married.

After all, how could they, when they both knew there was no real wedding night ahead of them and that this would all be over as soon as the weather cleared enough for Ryan to get her and the girls out of there.

But it was clear the girls had totally bought into the idea of Grace and Ryan living happily ever after in serenely wedded bliss, even if he and Grace weren't really sure what to do next during the "reception" part of the evening.

Fortunately the girls had plenty of ideas. "We want to take your picture!" Hannah announced.

"Smile!" Darlene urged cheerfully, aiming the camera she'd brought to record the high points of their field trip.

"Ms. Tennessen?" Letticia asked. "Are we s-s-supposed to call you Ms. McCoy now or Ms. Tennessen-McCoy?"

Grace knelt to hug the shy six-year-old, who Ryan couldn't help but note was stuttering a little less as she became more comfortable in her surroundings. "Either one will do, sweetie, or you can still call me Ms. Tennessen."

"At least until you get used to her new name," Ryan said, with a pointed glance in the direction of one of the listening devices.

Reminded of the ruse they were playing out, Grace started slightly then smiled. "Right," she agreed.

Ryan tossed her a wry smile, then leaned in close to wrap an arm about her shoulders and press a light kiss to her flushed cheek. "Remember, do everything you can to make this look absolutely authentic," he whispered in her ear. "Our safety here depends on it."

As if she didn't know that? Grace thought, exasperated. They'd been married less than ten minutes, and Ryan was already trying to call all the shots.

"You two stay right here, while we bring in your wedding dinner," Hannah said.

Grace blanched. She'd been so intent on working out the details of their impromptu wedding, she'd forgotten all about the evening meal. It wasn't like her to get so easily sidetracked. But then, her decidedly sensual response to Ryan wasn't like her, either. She bit her lip. "Oh, dear. I'm afraid there is no dinner, at least not yet."

Once again, the girls exchanged sly grins. "Oh yes there is, Ms. Tennessen," Greta announced.

Brianna took her thumb out of her mouth long enough to say, "'Cause we took care of it while you and Ryan were getting dressed." That said, the girls rushed out, and returned with a platter of fresh fruit, cheese and crackers. They insisted on waiting on Grace and Ryan hand and foot, and then they all sat around the fire and munched on the light but nutritious dinner.

"So what are you going to do about your job at the school?" Clara asked worriedly, as outside the snow continued to fall at a slow but steady rate, adding to the accumulation already on the ground. "I mean, now that you're married, are you going to quit?" she persisted worriedly.

"No," Grace said firmly, resisting the urge to fantasize about what it really might be like to be married to Ryan, and making plans about their future. She met the girls' glances reassuringly. "I'm not quitting."

Polly and the others considered this for a moment before Polly finally asked, "Is Ryan going to live with you, then?"

Good question, Grace thought as she looked at Ryan, who in turn glanced in the direction of the listening device, reminding her once again to watch what she said. "Yes, he will," Grace said firmly, and was rewarded by Ryan's smile.

"After all, when it comes down to it, I can really write songs anywhere," Ryan said.

But he couldn't be an agent for the Bureau just anywhere, Grace thought. To do that, he had to go where they needed him, wherever they needed him, even if it was far away from his family and far away from Grace.

Nevertheless, Grace thought, they could still enjoy the time they had together. And, she thought wryly, she intended to do just that.

"We're having hot chocolate instead of champagne,'' Darlene said. "On account of one, we don't have any and two, we're not old enough to drink.''

"We sort of had to improvise when it came to a wedding cake,'' the girls said, as they carried in a slightly lopsided three-layer creation with a great deal of hoopla. "'Cause, of course, there was no time to bake one. Luckily Ryan had somethin' we could use in the freezer.''

Brianna cupped her mouth with her hands as she informed in a stage whisper, "It's Hostess Twinkies covered with Cool Whip.''

Grace and Ryan both grinned at the girls' ingenuity.

"It's okay, though,'' Hannah told them cheerfully, before they could comment. "You can still cut it.''

"Yeah, you gotta have pictures feeding each other cake for your wedding album,'' Darlene said.

Ryan glanced at Grace as if there were nothing he'd rather do more than spend time with her indulging in every hedonistic delight imaginable. "I'm game if you are,'' he drawled.

Grace blushed a self-conscious pink despite herself. She wondered what else he was game for, then decided she didn't want to know. "Of course I am.'' She ignored her racing pulse and smiled at the girls. "I wouldn't miss this homemade cake for the world.''

Together, she and Ryan cut the cake. Ryan picked up the larger section of cream-filled sponge cake covered in whipped topping and lifted it toward her lips. The girls laughed as he playfully coaxed it between Grace's lips, then slowly stroked the excess off with the pads of his fingers. By the time he'd finished, she was hot and tingly all over. Which—all things considered—was definitely not fair.

"Your turn," Grace said, determined to give as good as she'd gotten.

As the girls grinned and oohed and aahed, she cut an even bigger piece of cream-topped and cream-filled Twinkie, and urged it between Ryan's lips. Instead of allowing her to slip away unscathed if she chose, he let his mouth close over her fingers. When she would have pulled away, he caught her hand in both of his, and—his eyes twinkling mischievously—held it there until he had personally kissed off every centimeter of the excess cake, cream filling and whipped cream.

"I've never seen anything so dreamy," Clara sighed.

And I've never felt anything so sensual! thought Grace.

"Speaking of dreams," Ryan said, clearing his throat, as he watched Letticia rub her eyes sleepily. "It's been a long, eventful day. Hadn't you girls better be going to bed?"

"Ooooooh!" the girls chorused, as Grace flushed all the more. "They want to be alone."

"Can you blame them?" Hannah shrugged.

Darlene nodded as she told the younger girls with all the knowing wisdom of an almost teenager, "It's their wedding night."

"Okay, we're going," Hannah said cheerfully, "but first we have to have a toast." She lifted her cup of hot chocolate, and all the others exuberantly followed suit. "To Grace and Ryan. May this marriage bring them all the love and happiness they deserve."

"THEY'RE ALL ASLEEP," Grace said, half an hour later.

While she had supervised the teeth brushing and good-nights, tucked the girls in and tidied the upstairs bathroom, Ryan had done the dishes and cleaned up the living room. Now, as the clock struck ten, she was still in her improvised wedding dress, and Ryan was still in his sport jacket and tie. And once again, Grace was left wondering what next. Would he kiss her again? Or considering the sparks that always seemed to ignite when they indulged in that particular activity, would Ryan do the smart and responsible thing and pass on more kissing altogether?

"Then it's our turn, isn't it?" he said, sweeping her up into his arms.

Grace gasped, trying hard not to imagine what it would be like to really be married to Ryan, to have him living with her in her apartment near the school. But this marriage wasn't real, she reminded herself severely, even if her *feelings* for Ryan were.

"What are you doing?" she demanded haughtily, trying to regain control of the situation once again.

Ryan grinned as he shifted her all the closer to his chest. His eyes held hers for a breath-stealing moment, before he aimed his voice at the nearest listening device. "I'm carrying you up to our bed."

Our bed, Grace thought. Not his. She gulped as she

used her hands to create more distance between them. "The girls—"

"Are sound asleep," Ryan whispered back, as he stopped moving and stood with his arms locked around her. "And if you're as quiet as I intend to be, they'll stay that way."

Ryan took the stairs, swept down the hall and into the bedroom. As he moved, Grace ignored the sudden tightness of her throat, as well as the possessive feel of his hands upon her. But there was no pretending that the hours ahead did not fill her with a mixture of elation and anticipation. Like it or not, she wanted to be alone with him. She wanted to see what the future held. Judging by his unrepentant grin, she had an idea about the depth of his physical passion for her, but she wanted to see just how deep his feelings for her went.

And maybe now at last she would know, she thought, as ever so gently, Ryan laid her on the bed. Her thighs were liquid, weak. She was hanging on to her self-control by a thread, when he then followed her down, stretched out over the length of her, and whispered in her ear.

"I've got to go out alone again," Ryan told her, in a deathly quiet voice the listening device that had been planted in their bedroom could not pick up. "Now— while it's still dark."

Chapter Eleven

Grace stared at him as if she couldn't believe her ears, and the romantic part of Ryan could hardly blame her. It was their wedding night, after all, and he was running out on her without so much as a tender, heartfelt kiss. But he knew he couldn't start kissing her right now, because if he started, this time he might not stop. "I'll be back as soon as I can," Ryan whispered in her ear, wishing like hell he hadn't had to hurt and disappoint her this way.

Grace clutched his arms and pressed her lips against his ear. "But if they see you—?"

Ryan pointed to the listening device that had been mounted in the bedroom. He wished he could throw that—and all the other bugs that had been planted in the house—out, but he knew he couldn't without putting them all in grave danger. "They won't suspect a thing as long as you make them think I'm very, very busy." As well he might have been, Ryan thought ruefully, had he been able to stay.

Grace swallowed and again touched her lips to his ear. "Be careful."

Ryan tried not to think how much her concern meant to him as he grinned and advised, his voice a little sharper than he intended, "Just stay calm and moan and sigh once in a while—" again he pointed to the bug "—until I get back."

"No problem," Grace whispered back as she reluctantly let him go.

"WELL, SOUNDS LIKE they're on to you," Juliet said as soon as Ryan had filled her in on what was happening. "At the very least damn suspicious."

Ryan frowned as he paced the interior of the surveillance room inside the cave. He lifted a hand to rub at the tense muscles in his neck, then looked into the telescope aimed at the Hindale farm. To his chagrin, many of the lights over there were still on, but it did not appear that there was any activity outside the farmhouse. "Hopefully, our marrying tonight allayed their suspicions somewhat."

"Speaking of that marriage—it was a brilliant move on your part."

Ryan smiled as he thought about what a beautiful bride Grace had been. "Thanks."

"And at the same time perhaps the most foolish thing you've ever done. If she'd been an agent, too, it would've been one thing, but an ordinary citizen, Ryan?" Juliet continued incredulously.

There was nothing ordinary about Grace, Ryan thought. She was the bravest, feistiest, most spectacular woman he'd ever known. Furthermore, she made him feel like no other woman ever had. When he kissed her, he felt increasingly complete, increasingly impatient for more. He wanted to make love to her, to know what it was like to wake up with Grace in his arms every single day. He wanted a future with her, the kind his work would not allow him to give her. And even though he knew he couldn't begin to give her the kind of attention and tender loving care she deserved, Ryan couldn't help but wish that would change.

"Grace was glad to do whatever was necessary," Ryan told Juliet gruffly.

Juliet sighed, then continued heavily, "Just make sure Ms. Tennessen knows that a ruse is all this marriage is."

Ryan uttered a curt sigh. "She knows, all right." Now, if only he could convince himself. Because there'd been a moment when it had seemed all too real, when they'd said their vows, when he could not only imagine her as his wife, but had wanted her to be his wife. Not just for tonight and tomorrow, but for all time. And if that wasn't lunacy, what was? Ryan asked himself grimly. A deep-undercover agent like him had no business getting married.

And that being the case, he had to be practical about this, whether he wanted to or not. He had to stop getting sidetracked by his growing feelings for Grace and concentrate on his job once again. "When can you get Grace and the girls out of here?" he asked his boss gruffly.

"I'll call the governor now and we'll get snow-plows and road salt up there by first light," Juliet promised. "The snowfall in your area is dying down again, so hopefully at least one lane down the mountain will be cleared by mid-morning. And Grace and the girls will simply be able to drive out as though nothing were wrong. It's the best we can do to get them out of harm's way without raising suspicion and blowing your cover. In the meantime you-all should be safe, as the military and the Bureau are going to be surrounding and closing in on the militia under cover of darkness tomorrow evening. Thanks to the surveillance photos you faxed to us, we were able to get warrants to arrest them for the theft of the two U.S. Army tanks."

"Just don't let Grace and the girls get hurt," Ryan said gruffly. He didn't know what he would do if anything happened to any of them.

"We'll do our best, but as you well know, their lives and yours aren't the only ones at stake here."

Ryan knew the Bureau had a responsibility to protect the government workers the militia had targeted, too. It didn't make his worry any less.

Figuring the least said on that score, the better, Ryan signed off. He took the secret passageway out of the surveillance room and left the cave. As he stepped out into the cold winter night, it was still snowing, though not as much. He figured by morning only another three inches or so would've been added to the record snowfall they'd already had.

Certain he hadn't been followed, he headed back for the farmhouse and slipped inside. Grace was upstairs in the bedroom, pacing back and forth, waiting for him, the folds of her lace-edged white negligee swirling seductively about her slender curves. She had taken her hair down and brushed it out to devastatingly sexy effect—it fell over her shoulders like a mantle of shimmering gold silk.

When she saw him, she made a soft sound of relief and delight, then went straight to him, took him into her arms, and hugged him fiercely.

Not, Ryan thought as he hugged her back just as fiercely, because their bedroom was still bugged, but because she was genuinely glad to see him. "I'm so glad you're back," she whispered in his ear. "I was so worried that you'd been hurt or captured or whatever it is groups like that do to people who are spying on them."

Ryan smiled down at her and pressed a light kiss to her lips. Wary of the listening device, Ryan gestured for her to join him in the unbugged master bath. He went inside, shut the door behind them and turned on the faucet in the sink to further mute everything they said.

"Everything's fine," he told Grace softly, wrapping his arms around her and holding her close. As she leaned against him, the warmth of her breasts molded softly to his chest. "They're getting the roads between here and town plowed at first light. You and the children should be able to drive out of here by noon. Once you get to town, there will be undercover federal agents waiting for you who'll escort you the rest of the way."

Abruptly the color drained from Grace's face. She

stepped back slightly. Her hands curled around his biceps as she looked up at him. "What about you?" she asked huskily.

"I'll be here doing surveillance and feeding it to the troops and agents moving in on Hindale and his cronies."

Grace swallowed and looked all the more distraught. "Which means you'll be in danger, too."

Ryan shrugged, knowing this was all a part of his work. "Not for much longer."

"But for a while," Grace insisted passionately as her face paled all the more and her lower lip began to tremble.

What could he say? He couldn't deny it. He wrapped a comforting arm about her shoulders. "You should get some sleep."

"No," Grace said. She studied him with eyes that were at once full of yearning and profoundly hopeful. "Sleep is not what I want."

Ryan smoothed the hair from her face as his heart began to pound. "Then…" He forced himself to hold off until she'd made her intentions clear.

"We only have a few hours left," she told him softly, as his eyes skimmed her face. "I don't want to spend the rest of my life regretting what might have been if only we'd been together," she told him in a voice that was stormy with desire. She thrust out her chin stubbornly. "I've already done that once," she announced passionately. "I'm *not* doing it again."

Just make sure she knows that a ruse is all it is, Juliet had said.

Knowing that, knowing he was working here, turning Grace down should have been easy; it wasn't. Especially when he could feel the strain of her body against his and knew she was aching to be touched. "Grace, our marriage wasn't real," he told her firmly. *Even if it felt like it was to him, too.*

"But my feelings for you are," Grace said softly in a low, sexy voice that ignited all his senses. She regarded him wantonly as she ran both her palms over the straining muscles of his chest.

"Make love to me, Ryan," she pleaded passionately. "Make this a night neither of us will ever forget."

Ryan stared at her. "You don't mean this," he said gruffly.

"The heck I don't!" Grace countered, just as emotionally. "I may not be all that experienced—"

Ryan groaned and looked all the more torn. "Don't remind me."

"But I'm a grown woman," Grace continued defiantly, determined to get her way on this no matter what she had to do. She wound her arms about his neck, the happiness within her brimming up unchecked. They might be together for only a moment in time, but what counted was that they had found each other at all.

"I know what I want," she told him softly as she pressed her lips to his, knowing she belonged in his arms and nowhere else, "and what I want is you."

Ryan tunneled his hands through her hair and kissed her with the same deep and abiding hunger she felt, until she moaned low in her throat and leaned against him weakly, until she wasn't the only one who felt they were both moving toward something they were incapable of stopping.

"Then that's what you'll get," he promised huskily, as he gently kissed her cheek. "But first—"

Releasing her wordlessly, Ryan slipped without a sound into the bedroom beyond. He removed the bug in the bedroom and, one finger pressed to his lip, brought it back into the bathroom. Ever so gently he set it down. A mischievous look on his face, he made some obnoxious snoring sounds for the benefit of anyone still listening.

Grace clapped a hand over her mouth to stifle a giggle.

Still snoring, he pushed her in the direction of the bedroom and quietly shut the bathroom door behind them.

They were alone in the darkened master bedroom. A single candle, throwing off a soothing vanilla scent, burned on the table next to the cozy double bed.

He tugged her toward him. "And now that that is taken care of," he whispered as he sifted his hands through her hair, over and over, until her heart was beating wildly, out of control. "On to better and better things." His mouth covered hers, demanding and receiving a response she hadn't realized she could give as she leaned against him, savoring his warmth and strength, even as she stroked the daunting width of his shoulders, the sinewy length of his arms and the powerful muscles in his chest and back.

He drew her closer still, getting to a place inside her where no one had ever touched. Her heart soaring, Grace found a comfort in the present, in him, that had never existed for her in the past. And might never exist again. Desire spreading like a fever deep inside her, she melted beneath his kiss, grateful for the giddiness even as she felt her knees weaken and her senses sharpen. Being with Ryan like this was everything she had ever dreamed, every fantasy she'd ever had.

The fact it wouldn't last hardly mattered, she thought, as his tongue slid between her lips to tease and touch and tempt her. She intended to savor every second of this, to warm her heart when she was alone again.

She arched against him, her mouth hungry, her breasts crushed against the powerful muscles of his chest. She was pulsing all over, inside and out. His hands splayed across her hips, lifting her against the rigid proof of his desire.

Enfolded against him, snuggled in his arms, emboldened by his kiss, Grace felt an excitement unlike any she had ever known. She wanted to yield to him and the need that drove them both.

Their love had descended upon them with the blinding, all-encompassing ferocity of the snowstorm. And though the blizzard would end, Grace sensed their feelings for each other...the union of souls they were experiencing now...never would. Trembling with excitement and need, she hiked the gown she'd been married in to her waist and started to shimmy out of her panties. "I want you."

A slow, knowing grin spread across his face.

"What I lack in experience I make up for in enthusiasm," Grace teased.

"That you do," Ryan whispered back. "And what a sexy and courageous woman you are," he said, as he hooked his hands beneath the elastic and helped skim them down her thighs.

His body throbbed as he looked his fill. Sweet, sexy thighs and a mound of golden curls. She was so warm and slender and her mouth was giving enough to push him over the edge of reason. Aware he'd never wanted anyone this wildly, aware he'd never had more reason to proceed with care, he kissed her until his blood swam and her breath came in jerks, until their tongues writhed like lovers locked together and the kisses flowed, one into yet another. And another....

He wanted this to be perfect for her, Ryan thought, as his own body voiced an equally urgent demand, and he lowered her to the bed. Whatever happened later between the two of them, he wanted it to be worth it.

"Ryan—" Grace's murmured word was half plea, half moan.

Determined not to rush this, he pushed the gown higher, above her breasts, and sucked her nipples through the thin lace of her bra. "You're not ready," he whispered.

She gasped as he unhooked the front clasp of her bra, and bent to take her in his mouth. She bucked and dug her hands in his hair. "I'll be the judge of that," she murmured breathlessly.

"No." He grinned, as he took in the unique floral

fragrance that was hers and slid down toward her thighs and spread them wide, "I will."

She might not have known what she'd been missing, but he did, and he was determined she experience it all before he caused her any pain; as hard as he was, he was bound to cause her some. He kissed her navel and the silky abdomen beneath. She moaned as his hot breath ghosted over her skin. Loving the feel of her, the soft, clean, sexy scent of her, he gently stroked the inside of her thighs.

"Ryan—"

"Nope," he whispered softly, knowing exactly what she needed, and exactly what she was going to say. Loving the feel of her, he let his lips move across her skin. "You're not. Because if you were—" he tucked a finger into her softness, and found it damp and hot and tight...too tight "—I'd know."

"But—" she protested, trembling, as his lips toured the inner softness of her thighs.

"Just lie back and close your eyes." Still stroking her gently, he waited until she did. "And let yourself go," he whispered, knowing she was at her most vulnerable, as he touched her with his lips and explored her with his hands, not stopping until she was silky wet and trembling.

"Like this?" she whispered, as she shuddered against his lips.

"Exactly like this," Ryan sighed contentedly as another bolt of fire cannoned into his groin and he shifted his body back up over hers. Eager to please her, he kissed her breasts until they were tight, aching peaks and her knees fell open even more.

"How about this?" Grace asked as his lips again returned to the boundless pleasures of her mouth. Ryan trembled as the softness of her hand curled around him, her aptitude for loving him no surprise. He'd known since he met her that he would never feel about another woman the way he felt about her.

He groaned. "This is good, too."

"And this?" She stroked him from base to tip until he damn near lost what little was left of what he considered to be almost superhuman restraint.

Unable to help himself, Ryan uttered a soft sound that was part chuckle, part moan. Damned if beneath all that ice Grace wasn't a wild woman, after all.

Angling his body against hers, he tested her readiness as he whispered against her lips, "Princess, you are every bit as sweet and sexy as I knew you'd be."

Grace rubbed the tips of her breasts against the soft hair on his chest, trusting him enough to let him know how much she wanted him. "Then love me, Ryan," she urged, returning his deep, devouring kisses with a sweet and tender wantonness all her own. "Love me now."

Unable to deny either of them the pinnacle of pleasure any longer, Ryan grasped her hips and lifted her to him. Their hearts thundered together as he pushed through the barrier of her innocence and, near to bursting, eased inside her.

He struggled to hold on to his composure. "This is

what you do to me," he told her, stroking her, soothing her and setting her ablaze.

"And this is what I want to do for you," he murmured as she made an impatient sound in the back of her throat and he began to move inside her, slowly, sensually, each thrust more forceful than the last, until her hips undulated beneath him.

Grace held him close, her arms cupping his shoulders. He responded by going even deeper, so deep she shuddered, as did he. Their mouths met in a long, soul-searching kiss, and for the first time in her life, Grace learned what it was like to be pampered and prized, what it was like to be with a man, body and soul, and to love him with every inch of her heart.

Love him so much that it no longer mattered to her what the future held. Ryan was all she cared about, she thought, as the pleasure gripped them both and sent them both skyrocketing over the edge. No matter what came of their marriage, she knew for her there would never be anyone else.

For long moments afterward they lay cuddled together, so still they might have been asleep. Eventually Grace turned her head and pressed a kiss into his throat. "Did I tell you," she murmured sleepily, holding him closer and exalting in all that they had shared, "that tonight has been the best, most exciting night of my life?"

"Mine, too," Ryan murmured as he drew her beneath him, framed her face with his hands and kissed her deeply once again. He had wanted her introduction to lovemaking to be nothing but the best. And it had been. "But it's not over yet." And if he had his way, he thought contentedly, it wouldn't be for some time to come.

Chapter Twelve

Ryan woke just after dawn to the sounds of the snow-plow and salt truck rumbling past on the road below. He got up from the bed and padded barefoot to the window. Easing the curtain aside, he saw that one lane was being cleared. Just that quickly his time with the woman he'd come to feel was his wife, in every respect that counted, was up.

But then, what had he expected, he wondered grimly, considering the sham marriage they had entered in.

"What's going on?" Grace asked sleepily behind him.

Working hard to curtail his emotions, Ryan let the curtain fall and reached for his jeans. "They're clearing the road."

Grace shoved the tangled hair from her face, the vulnerability in her expression as clear as the disappointment in his heart. She drew a breath. Her tongue snaked out to wet her lips. "It's stopped snowing?"

Ryan's lips compressed. "Yep," he said curtly, trying not to notice how deliciously tousled she looked, or how well loved.

Grace's face fell as she tugged the sheet up over her breasts. It was all Ryan could do to restrain himself from making hot, wild, passionate love to her again.

He sat down on the edge of the bed, knowing that as much as he would have liked to relax and enjoy the morning after, it would be too dangerous. He had a job to do now. "The sooner we get you and the girls out of here, the better."

She swallowed and fitted her smaller trembling hand in his larger one. "You really think we're in danger?"

This was no time to sugar coat things. Ryan nodded. He wished he could attend only to Grace now, but he knew he couldn't. He inclined his head in the direction of the two rooms where the girls were sleeping. "You better wake them up and get them dressed and packed." To stop himself from kissing her, he moved away from the bed.

Grace got up, dragging the sheet with her. She followed him over to the chair while he sat down and tugged on his socks and boots. When he stood, her arms went around him to hold him close. "Are you going with us?"

Ryan drank in the scents of sleep and sex. As the sheet shifted and fell to her waist, her breasts were pressed against his bare chest. Wishing he could do a helluva lot more than just offer assistance, he smoothed a hand down the silky skin of her back. "I'll take you as far as town," he promised gently.

Despite his reassurance, apprehension glimmered in her jade green eyes. "But then you're coming back?"

"I have to, Grace," Ryan told her gruffly. Reluctantly he unfastened her arms from around his middle. He knew it had been a mistake to touch her—all he wanted now was to hold her and love her—but he couldn't keep her or the others safe that way. The only way to do that was to divorce his emotions from the situation—immediately!

His temper simmering—that fate had him leaving the love of his life so soon after he'd found her—he stepped away from Grace and, still scowling unhappily, snatched up his clothes. "It's my job, Grace." He shrugged on his shirt and buttoned it up the front.

Grace studied him for what seemed an eternity as he buttoned, tucked, zipped and buckled. Finally she drew the sheet back over her nakedness. Her chin high, eyes shimmering with hurt, she said quietly, "I'll call the headmistress and tell her we're going to try and leave."

Ryan nodded. There would be time to tell her how much he loved her. How much he wanted their marriage to become a real one, in every respect. But not now, when—due to the grim precariousness of the situation—everything was rushed. "All right," he said.

Grace drew a deep, bracing breath and picked up the phone on the bedside table. Already dialing, she lifted it to her ear. Her expression perplexed, she depressed the button, listened, depressed it again.

Her face losing all color, she turned to him in alarm. "Ryan—the line's dead."

At Grace's announcement, any number of swear words came to Ryan's mind. He wordlessly took the receiver from her and picked up the base of the phone. He examined both, to make sure the cords were plugged in the way they should be. Finding nothing amiss there, he traced the cord to the wall. Again, all was in order.

Grace's eyes widened. Her hand flew to her chest. "You don't think—"

Though Ryan would've done anything to spare Grace pain or fear, now was not the time to be less than forthright with her. Chances were, this was no accident. Still— "The snowstorm last night could've disabled the line," he told her calmly.

Grace swallowed as the panic in her began to build. Her hands clutched the sheet until her knuckles turned white. A pulse throbbing in her neck, she edged closer. "And if it didn't? There's been no trouble with the lines when the blizzard was in full force."

Ryan swung his gaze back to her. "Then Hindale has tampered with the lines in the area, to cut off communication between here and town," he said very quietly.

That was all it took for Grace to pull herself together. She tossed the sheet back onto the bed and quickly began to dress in her warmest clothing. Her face was as white as the snow outside but her actions were calm, methodical. Ryan realized with relief he could count on her to keep her head in even the most demanding, dangerous situations. And that was good, he thought, as he stepped into the closet. He rummaged around beneath a pile of sweaters and carried out a locked metal box. While Grace finished dressing, he swiftly worked the combination, and pulled a gun and shoulder holster from it.

Grace watched him load it and put the safety on, before he secured it in his holster and shrugged on a down vest that effectively hid both.

"I'm going outside to have a look around."

Fully dressed now, and in tight control of her emotions, she crossed the distance between them swiftly and gave him a hug. "Be careful," she whispered fiercely.

Ryan nodded, his mood remote and tense, the way it always was when a situation started to go sour. "I will," he said, as he returned her embrace cursorily and moved her away from him, knowing even if she didn't that he was the target here.

A pulse beat of silence fell between them, more distancing than any words.

Grace looked at Ryan as if he were a stranger to her. "What about the bugs downstairs?" she asked quietly. The one they'd moved out of their bedroom was still in the master bathroom and safely out of transmitting range of where they were standing now, but the rest of the house was filled with them.

"I'll leave them up."

Grace nodded, wordlessly agreeing with his assessment that that course posed less of a risk. And yet she had her concerns, too, he noted, as she folded her arms in front of her, lifted her chin and trained her wary jade green eyes on his.

"The girls are going to want an explanation as to why we're leaving so suddenly."

Especially after last night, Ryan thought.

Grace's lips tightened and she looked up at him as if their impromptu marriage and night of bliss had never happened. As if the two of them were strangers, still. "What should I tell them?" Grace demanded in a low, tormented voice.

Make something up, Ryan wanted to say, but he knew it was unfair to leave the fabrication up to her. He shrugged his broad shoulders aimlessly and strapped another gun into his boot. "Tell them that as pleasant as your sojourn here has been, the blizzard is over, and it's time for you to get them back to school."

Grace rubbed the chill from her arms and kept her eyes trained on his. "They're going to want to know why you're not going with us," she reminded him with a cool practicality that set his teeth on edge.

So will Hindale, Ryan thought as his whole body tensed with the need to protect her. "Tell them I have to close the farmhouse up and get the utilities turned off, but that I'm going to follow you in a few days, or as soon as I can." It was the best story he could come up with on such short notice.

"Right," Grace replied dutifully enough, but as he looked into her eyes one last time before rushing out the door, he noted she had tagged this as the kind of kiss-off she'd suffered through before, from both her parents and her former fiancé, and had no wish to endure again.

To Grace's chagrin, rousing the girls was every bit as difficult as she had expected it might be. They were exhausted from both their play in the snow and the wedding, and wanted only to snuggle in their cozy, down-filled Peach Blossom Academy sleeping bags.

"We're leaving before breakfast?" Hannah asked as she stood rubbing the sleep from her eyes.

"How come?" Clara asked as she, too, struggled to her feet.

Grace went into teacher mode. "Because it's stopped snowing and the snowplows have cleared the road."

"Is Ryan coming with us?"

Grace shook her head. "No. I don't think so," she told the girls, smiling briskly.

"How come?"

Grace pushed away the suspicion that all was not right with the two of them, and forced herself to concentrate on the dead phone. And the fact it could be a fluke, or it could be a portent of utter disaster and extreme danger. "He has things to do here," she said as she helped the two youngest children, Brianna and Letticia, dress quickly.

"Did you two have a fight last night?" Greta asked, keying in to the urgency driving Grace and picking up the pace along with everyone else.

"No." Grace replied, as she began packing up suitcases, too. "What would make you ask that?"

"You look funny," Hannah replied as she shrugged on her tailored slacks with the Peach Blossom Academy insignia. "All worried or something."

"Yeah," Polly chimed in, pigtails bobbing. "What's up?"

Grace forced a carefree smile. "Nothing's up. We just have to leave. And I want to get an early start before it begins snowing or something, or heaven forbid the roads freeze over."

Alas, they knew her too well to buy it. Grace had been wearing her heart on her sleeve the past two days; hence, her love for Ryan was obvious to them all. Just as her fear that last night hadn't meant nearly as much to him as it had to her was now obvious as well.

Ryan had loved being her first, and he had loved making love to her. But, now, in the cold light of day, he was tense and grim and emotionally remote, and obviously having regrets about getting so close to her so quickly.

He didn't want to tell her that yet, of course, being the gentleman he was at heart. But as soon as this was over, as soon as she got the girls to safety and he wrapped up his case for the Bureau, she had the sinking feeling that the kiss-off speech she had half expected all along would be delivered posthaste.

And breaking heart or no, Grace was going to have to find a way to handle it.

Brianna took her thumb out of her mouth. She marched up to Grace. "I want to talk to Ryan."

Grace blocked the way to the stairs. There were fewer listening devices on the second floor, but the downstairs had enough to pick up conversation everywhere.

"You can't do that," Grace said in exasperation, as she made a motion for the other girls to hurry up, too. She breathed a sigh of relief as everyone finished putting on their socks and boots. "Why not?" Greta asked suspiciously.

Grace gathered up coats and mittens and began sending the girls to the bathroom. "Because he went out to the barn to get the truck warmed up for us."

Hannah's eyes narrowed. "There's something going on here."

"Yeah," they chorused, all in agreement. "What aren't you telling us?" Darlene asked.

RYAN LEFT THE BARN DOORS wide open, to keep carbon monoxide from accumulating inside the barn, and went straight to where Grace's truck was parked. He turned the ignition. Nothing. Frowning, he turned it again. Nothing. Not so much as a click. He swore, realizing the battery was dead, probably due to the combined factors that it hadn't been run in over twenty-four hours and it had gotten extremely cold last night.

Praying this was not uniformly the case, he leaped out of the driver's seat and went over to his pickup truck. He knew his vehicle should start, as he'd put in a battery designed to tolerate temperatures well below zero. Nevertheless, the first try yielded only a half-hearted rumble from the motor. On the second, the engine turned over. Ryan pressed down on the accelerator and revved the engine up even more. He waited until he was sure his pickup was not going to die on him and climbed back out.

He'd have to wait a few minutes, he thought, before he attempted to jump Grace's battery with his own. He left his still-running pickup truck and strode across the barn to find the jumper cables. He needed to get Grace's truck going and get her and the girls out of here.

"They're almost ready," Grace reported breathlessly a few minutes later as she dashed into the barn, lugging her own suitcase.

Ryan wanted nothing more at that moment than to take Grace on an extended honeymoon. But he knew for all their sakes that he had to concentrate solely on protecting her and her students.

"Good." His attention focused solely on his task, Ryan hooked up the jumper cables. While she watched, he climbed behind the steering wheel. To his immense relief, this time he started Grace's truck with no problem.

Grace set down her bag and watched as he stepped back out. Her face was pale with fear, her cheeks pink with exertion. Once again it was all Ryan could do not to drag her into his arms and kiss her until the night before felt like just a preamble to the passion- and love-filled lifetime ahead of them.

"I don't want to leave you here," she whispered.

Knowing he couldn't afford the diversion, Ryan climbed up into the loft. "I'll be fine," he told Grace, who was right behind him as he hunted around until he found a pair of high-powered binoculars, hidden in the hay. Still keeping his attention focused solely on his work, Ryan slid a loose wooden board slightly to the left, revealing a narrow slice of cloudy gray sky.

Grace crossed the loft to his side. She looked panicky as she curved a staying hand around his biceps. "It's dangerous."

Ryan focused on the snow-covered fields surrounding his farm and was relieved to see nothing but snow and trees. "Danger is all part and parcel of my line of work. I'm trained for this, Grace."

"I know that." Grace tugged on his sleeve imploringly. "Just the same. Promise me you won't take any chances," she whispered.

Ryan turned to her, loving her with all his heart and soul, but not about to let her hamstring him this way. Being an agent for the Bureau was as much a part of him as the color of his hair and eyes. And that part of his life wasn't going to change no matter who he got involved with. It was important she understand that. "I'll do what I need to do to get the job done." No more, no less, that was just the way it was.

She studied him with chin high and her shoulders squared. "Damn it, Ryan, don't you understand?" she whispered hoarsely as she shoved an impatient hand through the wind-tossed layers of her hair. "I don't want you hurt."

He touched her face. He wanted to tell her he loved her so badly, but knew this was not the time for an in-depth discussion of the relationship between them that had happened far too fast. Like it or not, they couldn't afford to indulge in their emotions now. His request they make this marriage a permanent one and his declaration of love—were both going to have to wait.

"I don't want you hurt, either," he told her gently, knowing this wild wanting he felt for her would never go away, no matter what happened next. "That's why I'm asking you to leave now," Ryan murmured as he went back to his cursory surveillance of his own property, then the Hindale farm.

"Damn," he said, as he picked up the first activity outside the farmhouse across the valley. *This was exactly what he'd been dreading.* The barn doors were swinging open. Twelve heavily armed men and women, dressed in combat fatigues, were pouring out.

Grace moved to his side once again, even as Ryan resisted the urge to gather her close and rest her head on his shoulder. "What is it?" she demanded, able to see it was something.

Ryan grimaced as he surveyed his opponents with a cold, hard stare. "They're getting out the stolen tanks." He watched a few seconds more. "And it looks like they're bringing them this way."

Grace would not have believed it if she hadn't seen it with her own eyes. She and Ryan were soon going to be under attack. Every protective instinct in her mobilized. "I've got to get the girls out of here," she said, her heart beating triple time.

Ryan caught her arm and swiftly pulled her back to him. "It's too late to take the truck down the road to town."

She stared up into his ruggedly handsome face but

didn't step away. "Why?" she asked incredulously, sure there must be a way out here, even if it wasn't immediately clear to her.

"Because they're splitting up. See?" Ryan handed her the binoculars and pointed out what he wanted her to see. "One tank is going down toward the bridge. The other is coming toward us."

Grace trained the binoculars in the direction he wanted and sucked in a breath. He was right—the tanks were both entering the meadow that separated the two farms. "Which means we're trapped," she said slowly.

"Right." Thank God the two stolen tanks weren't moving all that fast, Ryan thought. They had time enough, just barely time enough, to make a partial escape.

He hustled her down the ladder, past the truck and out the entrance of the barn in the direction of the farmhouse, where seven faces stood pressed against the windows, watching their every move.

"You're going to have to get the girls and take them through the woods to the cave," Ryan ordered gruffly, accompanying her across the yard. "You'll be safe there until help arrives."

"What about you?" Grace asked uneasily, still wishing fervently he'd change his mind and go with them.

Ryan gripped her shoulders. "If they've been listening to the devices they planted inside the farmhouse, and my guess is they have," he told her in a low bracing tone, "they're expecting your truck to leave, with you and the girls in it momentarily."

"So?" Grace said, ready to mutiny on a moment's notice, if it meant they would *all* be safe.

"So, your truck is going to leave, all right," Ryan announced emphatically, his jaw hardening. "Only, I'm going to be in it."

Grace blew out a shuddering breath as she realized he was going to set himself up to take the brunt of the attack, rather than attempt to get away with them. "Ryan, no—" she gasped.

"Don't argue with me, Grace." Turning his attention to the farmhouse, Ryan waved the girls on out. They spilled out the back door and ran toward them, en masse. As soon as they were within earshot, he began snapping out orders left and right. "Girls, there's no time for questions. We're in a bit of an emergency here, and I want you all to be quiet as mice and to go with Grace. She's going to take you through the woods to a secret place of mine. And I'll meet with you there later, okay? Meantime, you've all got to hurry as fast as you can. Nod if you understand." Their faces somber, they did.

"Good." Ryan breathed a sigh of relief as he turned back to Grace and finished issuing instructions in the same calm, commanding tone. "I want you to get on the phone as soon as you get to the cave and dial 'Achy Breaky Heart.' It's a secure line and it'll put you in touch with Juliet, my boss. Give her this message. Tell her 'Romeo's in trouble, and send in the big guns now.' Got that?"

Grace nodded. "Yes."

"Good. Juliet'll know what to do. Ten to one, we'll have both U.S. Military and Bureau choppers in the area within minutes." Ryan grabbed Grace and planted a quick, fierce kiss on her lips. "Now go," he ordered gruffly. "And don't look back."

Together, Grace and the girls dashed through the woods and into the cave. Grace found the button, opened the door to the surveillance room. Admonishing the girls to move quickly, she ushered everyone inside and quickly shut and locked the door behind them. Praying all the while she was not too late, she got on the phone, dialed "Achy Breaky Heart" and was promptly patched through to someone named Juliet. "This is Grace Tennessen. Romeo's in trouble. Send in the big guns now."

"Hold tight, Grace," Juliet snapped back. "We'll get there as soon as we can."

Her hands trembling badly, Grace hung up to find the girls surveying all the high-tech equipment with the same awe she had initially.

"Look, Ms. Tennessen-McCoy," Brianna pointed out. "Your truck is on that television screen."

"Yeah, it's going down the mountain," Hannah said, as everyone gathered around.

"Hey! Look at that snow popping up around it."

"What is that, anyway?"

"Oh my gosh—"

"Are those...bullets doing that?"

Grace paled at the sight of Ryan behind the wheel.

He ducked down as the truck careened around the curve, out of sight.

More snow went flying, as the tank came into view and a shower of bullets followed the path of the truck, which abruptly came back into view as it negotiated yet another hairpin turn on the curvy mountain highway.

"I can't see Ryan!" Hannah gasped.

"He's not turning the wheel!" Greta yelled. "Turn, turn! Get out of the way, Ryan!" they all screamed in unison. "Get out of the way!"

But he didn't turn the wheel, and to Grace's and the girls' horror, he didn't get out of the way. The truck kept going straight even as the road took another wicked turn. Grace and the girls gasped in horror as the truck flew over the cliff at deathly speed and hurtled down...down...into the snowy valley below.

Silence fell in the surveillance room as they all stared in shock at the screen, none of them able to believe what they had just seen.

Seconds later a number of helicopters came into view. And amazingly, more tanks from the opposite direction—legitimate ones. A whole line of them.

Almost before they knew what had happened, the two tanks from the Hindale farm were surrounded.

"Are the bad people going to surrender?" Hannah asked, as the girls crowded closer and clung to Grace.

"I don't think they have any choice," Grace murmured, still watching the monitor as the militia members began to emerge from the opening of the tanks, their hands held high over their heads.

"But what about Ryan?" Darlene whispered, upset.

"Is he okay, do you think?" Greta breathed.

Grace drew a jerky breath and laid a hand across her heart. He couldn't have gone over the side of the mountain. It just was not possible. Ryan was smarter than that. More skilled in surviving. For heaven's sake, he did this for a living! "He's okay," she said firmly, working hard to keep the edge of hysteria out of her voice. *He has to be okay. Please, dear heaven, he has to be.* After all, she'd know it if he were dead, wouldn't she? Wouldn't she?

Without warning the door to the secret surveillance room slid open behind them. A snow-covered man who looked as though he had just stepped out of a tundra stood in front of them.

For the hundredth time in two minutes, the girls shrieked, squealed and screamed, but this time Grace didn't mind as she let out a joyous whoop and launched herself into the intruder's snowy arms.

"Ryan!" Brianna came up from behind and clasped Ryan around the knees.

"You're okay!" Hannah said as she joined the group hug.

"You d-didn't die!" Letticia did the same.

"We love you, Ryan," Polly cried, piling on, too.

"And we're so glad you're okay," Darlene enthused.

Tears streamed down Grace's face as Ryan hugged them all, while on the monitor screen Hindale and his cronies climbed from the tanks and surrendered to the soldiers and Federal agents surrounding them.

"What happened to you?" Clara demanded.

"Well, as you can see, I didn't die," Ryan murmured huskily, tongue in cheek, "but I did dive headfirst into a snowbank."

Grace had never been more frightened than she had been as she'd watched the truck she'd thought was still carrying him go over the cliff.

"I don't care how you did it," she confessed huskily, burying her face in his shoulder as tears of joy streamed down her face. "I'm just glad you're here."

"We all are," a low and sexy woman's voice said.

In unison, Grace and Ryan turned to face the attractive, gun-toting woman framed in the doorway and the Federal agents wearing boldly lettered Bureau of Domestic Antiterrorism Activity jackets on either side of her.

Ryan regarded her with a mixture of relief and happiness. He raised a lazy hand. "Hey, there, Juliet."

"Oh, Romeo." Juliet smiled back. "Achy Breaky Heart or not, it's good to finally see you again."

Chapter Thirteen

Seven hours later Ryan stood framed in the doorway of the conference room back at Bureau headquarters. Despite the night almost without sleep, his record-breaking trek through the snow to the cave and his near-fatal escape, Grace thought he looked strong, confident and at ease in a way that he never had when he was posing as an aspiring country-and-western singer. Free to act like the Federal agent he was, he was very much in his element. Whereas she, Grace thought uneasily, had never felt more like a fish out of water. She'd wanted only to cut the debriefing short so she could be with Ryan, but as she looked at his face she realized he clearly had his work on his mind and little else. Disappointment flowed through her, as fierce and unstoppable as the crest on a rising river.

"The bus is here to take you and the girls back to The Peach Blossom Academy," he announced. "Juliet and another agent are rounding them up now."

Grace nodded her understanding. Her heart pounding, she stood, too. She hadn't expected to feel so awkward around him, once they were all out of dan-

ger, but she did. And to her dismay, she sensed—
though he was probably too proud to admit it—that he
felt just as awkward around her.

Not that this should be a surprise to either of them,
Grace acknowledged in grim silence. She and Ryan
had been through every kind of fantasy the past couple
of days and lived them out to the max, but now they
were back to the real world and their real lives, and
they'd landed with a crash.

Thank heaven she still had her pride, too!

Determined not to let him see her pain and confusion, she forced a brisk smile. "Thanks for seeing that
the girls got pizza for lunch, free telephone calls to
their parents, and had a Disney movie to watch while
they waited for other transportation arrangements to
be made." He had even thoughtfully provided a small
amphitheater for the girls and their Bureau-employed
chaperones to use, while Grace was interviewed sep-
arately about all she had seen and heard, and then left
alone to wait for Ryan.

He shut the door behind him and, golden-brown
eyes holding hers, advanced on her slowly. "I wanted
to make sure you-all had everything you needed,"
Ryan said with a soft efficiency that sent tremors
through her.

Grace's eyes lifted to his. Without warning, her
heart began to pound and she knew this was it—the
moment of reckoning she both welcomed and dreaded.

"Thanks to you, we do," Grace replied. And thanks
to him, she also had finally experienced for the first

and only time in her life, what it was like to love and be loved in return, even if it was only for a little while.

"You've been a real trouper through all of this," Ryan said, lavishing praise on her as he pressed a light, cursory kiss on her brow.

Was he talking about her courage or their marriage? Grace wondered, wishing everything weren't so damn complicated. Unfortunately, there was no easy way to tell what Ryan was feeling, except relief that it was all over and that he could finally stop pretending to be an aspiring—though supremely untalented—country-and-western star and come down off that mountaintop. "I didn't have much choice, thrown into it the way I was," Grace told him quietly.

Ryan shook his head, admiration shining in his eyes. "Not every woman would have married an agent as part of the cover."

Was that all it had been? Grace wondered, all the more upset. *Part of the cover?* And yet, how could she realistically expect it to have been anything but that? People did not meet and fall in love and marry in the space of just three days and two nights. Not and expect it to last.

"Or slept with him, you mean," Grace interjected miserably.

Ryan blinked. A second later his composure was back. "That's not what I said," he returned evenly.

"No, of course not," Grace replied as she looked down at the cup of lukewarm coffee she held cradled in her hands. "You're too much of a gentleman to ever say anything that crude." That was one of the things she loved about him, and she did love him with all her heart and soul.

"But I'm not too much of a gentleman to think it, is that it?" Ryan demanded, his jaw set.

Grace shrugged with an insouciance she couldn't begin to feel and forced herself to look into his eyes. "Why not admit it? We're at a turning point here, Ryan." And just because she loved Ryan did not mean he loved her.

The truth was she'd let her heart guide her the past few days, instead of her head. But they weren't on some beautiful mountaintop in rural Virginia, caught in the throes of a record blizzard anymore. They were back in the real world, and this time she needed to make the right decision, one that would serve them well over all the years to come, instead of living in the moment and behaving like a lovestruck bride on her honeymoon. "We need to forget the games we were playing to add authenticity to your cover and be realistic again."

"Is that what this was to you?" he asked quietly, clearly not believing it for an instant. "Games?"

"Not all," Grace returned, just as quietly, as her stomach fluttered with a thousand butterflies. "There were parts of it, as you very well know, that I enjoyed," she admitted.

The guilt he felt over having bedded her, when he knew she was saving herself for marriage, flashed in his eyes.

"But good—no, let's be honest—great lovemaking does not make a marriage," Grace continued sagely, as she moved to the other side of the conference table and set her coffee cup down.

Ryan's eyes narrowed as he raked a hand through the wind-tossed layers of his hair. "Then what does?" he demanded impatiently.

"That's just it!" Grace cried, upset, as she flung her hands up in front of her. "I don't know and I don't think you do, either!"

Ryan swept around the table to her side. "Grace—"

Grace put up a hand to stop whatever he was going to say. "You don't have to say anything more." She'd been shunted to the side by her parents, more times than she could count, all in the name of duty. Her former fiancé had preferred fulfilling his duty as a career officer in the military to marrying her, too. Had Seth lived, who knew how long he would've put off their nuptials? She couldn't bear to be an impediment to his career or a burden to Ryan, too.

Tears stung her eyes as she backed up until her spine hit the wall. "I know you were just doing your job. And now your job is over, and you want to wrap things up and end our farce of a marriage." Grace took a deep breath, blinked away the unshed tears and pulled herself together. "It's perfectly understandable. And practical, too, now that there's no longer any compelling reason for us to play house."

Ryan studied Grace. He didn't know what had happened to her in the three hours or so they'd been apart, but she was acting as if the love affair between them had never happened. And there had to be a reason for that. He reached for her hand. "What did your head-mistress say about our marriage?"

Grace swallowed and extricated her hand from his. "I haven't told her yet."

Numb with disappointment and disillusionment, Ryan fastened his eyes on hers and struggled to contain his hurt. "I can see where it'd be a difficult thing to explain," he said quietly.

Especially since she and Ryan were not—as Grace had fervently hoped—going to stay married. Grace swallowed. "The important thing is the girls are safe and lives were saved all around. I don't think what I did to help you will be a problem."

Ryan moved toward Grace, his actions as confrontational and deliberate as hers had been evasive. "Look, I know things happened awfully fast—"

"That's an understatement, don't you think?"

He ignored her sarcasm and looked deep into her eyes. The situation was bad, but not unsalvageable, and it wouldn't be unless he lost his head. "But what we shared does not have to end on such a sour note," he told her firmly.

Grace's chin shot up. She regarded him with a combination of suspicion and hope. "What do you mean?"

"Unfortunately, there's no way around it." Ryan sighed heavily, wishing this were not the case. "I'm going to be busy here for the next several days, giving depositions and filling out reports on Hindale and his cronies. But," he lowered his voice to a gentle murmur, "I'd like to see you again when I'm free."

She swallowed around the lump in her throat and marshaled her defenses. "I don't think that's wise, do you?"

Because she looked like she was going to run away from him again, Ryan leaned in closer and braced a hand on the wall on either side of her.

Grace turned her face away from him stubbornly.

Silence fell between them as Ryan searched for a way to mend the rift that had come between them as soon as they returned to civilization. "I never meant to hurt you," he said quietly. He'd never forgive himself if he had.

Grace's lower lip trembled as she forced herself to look at him again and admit, "I know that."

"But?" He gave her a long look, his expression stony, and waited for the rest, which, judging by the recklessly independent tilt of her chin, promised to be more damning yet.

"You don't have to feel guilty, Ryan," Grace told him softly, abruptly becoming the warm, giving woman he had fallen in love with, married and made wild, wonderful love to throughout the night. "I wanted it to happen. I wanted us to make love."

"So did I," Ryan exclaimed heatedly as he began to take her in his arms.

"But now it's over," Grace told him emphatically, as the vulnerability faded from her eyes as suddenly as it had appeared, and her lips took on a firm, pouty line. He felt her start to tremble as she pulled away. "I've had the fling I've always wanted," she announced, taking several brisk steps away from him.

"And you successfully put Hindale and his cronies out of business and wrapped up your case. We have to get on with our lives."

And maybe, Ryan thought acerbically, if she said that enough out loud, she would actually start to believe it. But there was no way he ever would. What they'd felt together was real. And it had been important—damned important, as a matter of fact. Grace was frightened now, confused. But her uncertainty would fade once they spent time together, alone, away from the pressures of her work and his.

"I've got time off coming to me. Several weeks as a matter of fact. We can spend that time together."

He had hoped this would be the olive branch that would turn the tide in their direction. Instead, she barely blinked. "Yes, we could, but then what?" Grace began to pace the room, as restless as a lioness in a cage. "You'll just get another assignment that will give you a whole new identity and put you deep undercover."

"Probably."

Jade green eyes glittering, she whirled to face him. "I can't live that way, Ryan. With you off doing heaven knows what, putting your life in danger. And me waiting somewhere on the sidelines alone, always waiting for the news that you aren't coming back to me, after all."

Ryan swallowed. This was it then? It was really going to be over, just like that? "I never made any secret of the fact I love my work with the Bureau," he reminded her grimly, unable and unwilling to throw it all away because of his job.

Grace fastened a soft, feminine hand on his arm. "I know you didn't," she said gently. "I'm the one with the problem here. I'm the one who can't take what you have to offer—at least not on any ongoing basis." *I'm the one who can't take being desired but not loved.*

"You're telling me you want to end this completely and never see each other again?" If so, he did not believe it.

Grace was silent a long moment. Finally she stepped away from him and took a deep, bracing breath. "You remember what you told me about your ex-fiancée? How the two of you got involved during an assignment, only to discover what you felt when you were both living undercover and in such danger did not exist when you returned to your normal lives? Well, maybe it's like that," Grace theorized with unbearable sadness. She closed her eyes tight, then opened them again. "Maybe it was everything. The blizzard, the adventure, the danger, the chemistry between us. Maybe it all worked together to make us think that—that there was more there than there really was."

In any case what he was offering her was not enough, Ryan realized with unbearable sadness and regret, and it never would be. To hell with the fact he had given her more of his heart and more of himself than he ever had in his life. "I wish I would've known that was all it was for you—for us—at the time," Ryan told her as his breath came shuddering out.

"Because if you had, you never would've made love to me," Grace guessed dispassionately as her face grew pale, her shoulders stiffer.

"No, I wouldn't have," Ryan confirmed harshly. He stared at her, his fury and helplessness mounting. "Not if I'd known."

"I DON'T GET IT, and I don't think anyone else does, either," Hannah said, after Grace had finished her careful explanation on the chartered bus back to The Peach Blossom Academy for Young Women.

"Yeah, how can you say your marriage was all pretend, to fool the bad guys on the Hindale farm?" Darlene protested.

Greta chimed in, "We saw the way Ryan looked at you and you looked at Ryan."

Grace flushed. "I admit we, um, felt a spark or two."

"You mean you liked each other?" Clara surmised.

"Yes." Grace sighed. *Very much, while our romance lasted.*

"Then why don't you still like each other?" Brianna removed her thumb from her mouth long enough to ask.

"Because now the case Ryan was working on is over," Grace explained.

"So what?" Polly said with a shrug. "We still like him."

Grace sighed. "I know you do, girls."

"We don't understand why you don't like him anymore," Polly persisted.

"I do, it's just different," Grace explained.

Seven girls studied her. "So you're telling us what you felt for him wasn't real because you knew you were helping the Bureau catch some bad guys?" Darlene asked eventually.

Grace nodded. "I wanted to protect you girls. Ryan and I both did. And we had to make it look good."

"Well, if that's the case, you really fooled us," Hannah said glumly, looking every bit as upset as the rest of the girls, "'cause we really felt you two were head over heels in love."

That was the problem, Grace thought, they all had.

"FOR SOMEONE WHO'S SET to leave on a three-week vacation you don't look very happy," Juliet said.

"Funny," Ryan replied irritably as he switched off his computer and took a sip of the cold, black coffee on his desk. "I don't recall asking you to comment on my mood."

Juliet smiled, came all the way into his office and shut the door behind her. "I'm doing so, anyway."

"Well, don't," Ryan said shortly, as he jerked loose the knot of his tie.

"You ought to feel great to be responsible for putting Hindale and his paramilitary group away."

"I'm happy."

"Right," Juliet said dryly as she watched him unbutton the top button on his shirt, kick back in his chair and prop his feet on the edge of his desk. "And that scowl on your face proves it."

Ryan grimaced. "And your point is—?"

"You haven't been happy since Grace Tennessen and the girls left here." Juliet folded her arms in front of her. "In fact, if I didn't know better, I'd think you miss them."

Ryan shrugged, not too proud to admit there was a grain of truth to that. "I got used to having them around."

"All of them?" Juliet queried lightly, concerned. "Or Grace in particular?"

Ryan cradled his coffee against his chest and favored his boss and friend with a warning look. "You're skating on thin ice here, Juliet."

"And you, Romeo, are head over heels in love with Ms. Grace Tennessen."

Ryan took a last sip of the bitter coffee and set it on his desk. "Where did you get that idea?"

"Oh, I don't know." Juliet waved her hand airily. "It probably has something to do with the fact that fifteen days have passed since you two tied the knot, and you've still made no effort to fill out the necessary paperwork to have the marriage annulled."

"The marriage wasn't legal. We had no blood tests, remember? For it to be legal, we would still have to have blood tests and show proof to the magistrate who married us in Blue Mountain Gap."

"Nonetheless, the marriage is still on the books and it could come back to haunt you and Grace should either of you ever *want* to marry again."

"Well, I'm not going to," Ryan said firmly. Once had been enough for him. He wasn't going to risk his heart, only to have it ripped to shreds again.

"Grace might want to, though," Juliet pointed out cagily as she took a seat on the edge of his desk.

Ryan's feet hit the floor with an irritated thud. "Did she say as much to you?"

"No, strangely enough, she didn't say anything to me at all about it, not one word. It's almost as if she doesn't really want to erase any connection between the two of you, either."

Ryan frowned. Unable to sit still a moment longer, he shot to his feet and began to pace. "You're wrong about that."

Juliet shook her head, clearly disagreeing. "I don't think so, Romeo."

"She made it clear before she left she didn't want to see me again."

"Then why didn't she jump at the opportunity to have your marriage annulled?" Juliet prodded smugly as she picked up a pencil and tapped it restlessly on the top of his desk. "On behalf of the Bureau I offered to take care of it for her, and all she said was she'd get back to me."

As that news sunk in, Ryan squared his shoulders and forced himself not to get his hopes up. He'd been unrealistically optimistic once; he wouldn't do it again. "Maybe she fully intends to get to it, and she's just been busy teaching," he theorized, staring down at the landscaped bushes and trees that surrounded the huge brick building.

Juliet dropped the pencil in her hand, rose lithely and walked over to the window to join him. "And maybe, like you, she doesn't really want to end whatever it is that happened between the two of you," she told him with conviction. "Maybe her feelings for you go a lot deeper than any of us first suspected."

GRACE WAS CURLED UP on her living room sofa, grading the history test she had given that morning, when she heard the strains of a guitar outside her apartment door. And soon after, an unmistakably off-pitch voice.

"Oh, my heart it done got broke,
One cold and wintry day,
When the beauty who said she'd be my love,
Got up and ran away-ay-ay-ay."

Grace opened her door. Ryan was standing just outside it, his guitar propped against his hip, a sexy smile on his face. Her heart pounded and her spirits soared at just the sight of him. But knowing full well he could simply be here about the annulment they still hadn't bothered to get, she forced herself not to get too excited.

She sauntered closer, rolled her eyes and said dryly, "You know that melody is not original, don't you?"

Ryan furrowed his brow. "Sure, it is," he argued lazily as a distinctly mischievous gleam came into his eyes. "I wrote the lyrics myself."

"That, I don't doubt for a second," Grace drawled right back, aware he'd never looked as handsome as he did that second, in his blue chambray shirt and jeans. "But the melody you're singing it to is 'The

Yellow Rose of Texas.'" Grace demonstrated by humming a few bars.

"Oh." Ryan shrugged one broad shoulder, dropped his guitar to the side and sauntered forward, like the hero in a Western movie come to claim his errant bride. He stopped when he was standing toe-to-toe with her and rubbed a hand across his freshly shaven jaw. "I thought it sounded a mite familiar, but I couldn't imagine why."

"Right," Grace murmured as her lips curved in a sardonic smile. "And if I believe that one, you probably have some swampland you'd like to sell me."

Several other doors opened. Residents peeked out. Eyebrows were raised. Ryan lifted his arms as if to say, "What can you do when your woman won't give you the time of day?" and gave them one of his trademark aw-shucks grins.

Blushing hotly, Grace grabbed Ryan's arm. "I think you better come in before you cause any more of a ruckus."

"Why, thank you ma'am." Ryan smiled and tipped his head at her, the passion he'd always felt for her gleaming in his eyes. "I think I'd like that."

Oh, I'm sure you will. The more telling thing was that she would like it, too.

Her heart pounding, she led him inside and shut the door behind them. Wishing that she had on something other than the peach-and-white-striped Academy sweats, she led him toward the cozy chintz sofa. Bending to clear away the papers she'd been grading, she made room for him to sit down beside her. "So what's up?'' she asked, deadpan, as he set his guitar aside and took a seat on the other end of the sofa. "Are you going off on assignment again?''

Ryan nodded. ''Yep,'' he said as he fixed her with an intent look, "and it's a mighty important one, too.''

"I see,'' Grace murmured as her heart sank. Foolishly she'd hoped he had just come to see her because he missed her. Instead, he was—just as she had initially feared—probably here about the annulment papers Juliet was insisting they both fill out, ASAP. She swallowed hard and struggled to contain her swirling emotions as she meshed her gaze with his. "Are you a country-and-western singer in every assignment you take?''

"Nope.'' Ryan's rugged features gentled reminiscingly as he confided, ''In fact, this is only the second one where I've used this disguise.''

"Really.'' Unable to bear talking about that, or thinking about all she'd lost when the two of them had ended their whirlwind marriage of convenience, Grace shot to her feet.

"The first being the one in Blue Mountain Gap, Virginia, where we met,'' Ryan continued as he stood, too.

"I remember,'' Grace muttered as she paced the small, femininely decorated living room. In fact, she'd be remembering for the rest of her life. She pivoted toward him and narrowed her eyes at him as her next idea hit. ''Don't tell me you're going undercover here in Arlington,'' she said.

"In a manner of speaking, actually I hope to be

doing just that very soon,'' Ryan told her as he laced his arms about her waist and dragged her against him. ''But it all depends on you.''

Grace's heart pounded at his proximity. And yet, as much as she loved feeling his arms around her again, as much as she wanted to be with him, she couldn't wear her heart on her sleeve any longer. ''I am not posing as the soon-to-be Mrs. Ryan McCoy again,'' she told him sternly as she flattened her hands across his chest and felt his heart beat strong and fast beneath her fingertips.

Ryan smiled as he gently caressed the side of her face. Framing her face with his hands, he tilted it beneath his. ''How about as my wife then?''

Grace shook her head and took a deep, cleansing breath. She wanted so much for them—marriage, children and everlasting love, but she wanted him to want them, too. And if he didn't...well, she just didn't see any hope for them at all. With a weary sigh, she reminded him sadly, ''Ryan, we already played this game—''

''Which is,'' Ryan interrupted, taking a deep, ragged breath, ''to my way of thinking, precisely where we went wrong.'' He searched her eyes. ''We made it a ruse to throw off the crooks instead of the real thing. So, I'm here to tell you I want to backtrack a bit and pick up from the place where we said our I do's.''

Grace gulped. ''You want another wedding night?''

His eyes gleamed mischievously as he lowered his lips to hers, slowly savoring every bit of anticipation. ''Don't you?''

Grace sucked in a tremulous breath. She knew she would never want another man as much as she wanted Ryan, but there had to be more than just physical passion and casual friendship involved. There had to be the depth of commitment that would last a lifetime. "I can't just pretend to love you again," she warned.

"Sweetheart, I don't want you to pretend anything anymore," Ryan told her gruffly as she wreathed her arms about his neck. He ran his hands through her hair and kissed her deeply. Lifting his mouth from hers, he looked into her eyes and murmured tenderly, "I want you to love me with all your heart and soul and let me love you back in the same all-or-nothing, gotta-have-you way."

Tears of happiness misted her eyes. Grace had to admit this sounded like a commitment to her. "Are you saying you want us to have a real marriage?" she gasped joyfully.

Ryan grinned, the affirmation already in his shrewdly direct eyes. "Don't you?" he teased.

"Yes. Oh, yes, I do."

They kissed again, sweetly, tenderly, then long and passionately. The next thing Grace knew they were in her bed, and Ryan was making her his wife all over again.

Afterward he held her cradled in his arms. Knowing she could handle anything life threw her way as long as she had his love and he had hers, Grace rested her face against his chest and sighed contentedly. "I suppose I'm going to have to get used to your absences."

Ryan stroked a hand down her back. "Only during

the workday. I've taken a job as an instructor. I'm going to teach the ins and outs of going undercover.''

As much as she wanted to be with Ryan, she didn't want him martyring himself on her account. ''You won't miss being on assignment?'' she asked cautiously.

Ryan grinned and stroked her hair. ''Not as much as I'd miss not seeing you.''

He lifted her against him, and they kissed again with a leisureliness and heat that promised another round of lovemaking very soon.

''So,'' Grace asked with a grin as she ran a hand down his chest, loving the way he felt, his warmth and his strength, ''where are we going to live?''

''Right here is fine, for now.'' Ryan captured her hand and rolled so she was beneath him. ''But I have a feeling we're going to need a much bigger place this time next year, so maybe we better think about building ourselves a home near here,'' he said as he kissed her bare shoulder, the dip at the center of her collarbone and caressed his way up her throat. ''You do want children, don't you?'' he murmured, as she arched against him hungrily, amazed to find they were both ready to love again.

Grace nodded, his hands teasing her breasts while she ran her palms down his thighs. ''As many as we can handle,'' she confessed.

''If I have my way,'' Ryan teased, as he began to kiss her in all the old, familiar, wonderful ways, ''by night's end, we'll already have a baby on the way.''

Grace sighed happily and fit her lips to his. ''Then

let's get started," she said, smiling, knowing that in her love for Ryan and his for her, she'd found everything life had to offer at long last. "'Cause I can't think of anything that would please me more."

Prepare yourself for the Harlequin American Romance Blizzard of 1998!

Question:

What happens when a runaway bride, a young mother and a schoolteacher on a field trip with seven little girls get stranded in a blizzard?

Answer:

Not to worry, they'll each have a hot-blooded man to wrap them in sizzling male heat till the thaw—and forever after!

This winter cozy up with **Cathy Gillen Thacker's** new trilogy of romantic comedies for a case of cabin fever you'll never want to cure.

BRIDES, BABIES & Blizzards

Snowbound Bride (#713)
February 1998

Hot Chocolate Honeymoon (#717)
March 1998

Snow Baby (#721)
April 1998

Available wherever Harlequin books are sold.

Take 4 bestselling love stories FREE

Plus get a FREE surprise gift!

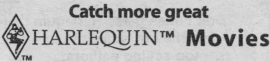

Don't miss these Harlequin favorites by some of our top-selling authors!